FUN & QUIRKY CLASSICS

Short Stories by Oscar Wilde, Mark Twain and More

Edited by Carolyn J. Wild

These stories are in the public domain.

The edits and layout of this book are

Copyright © 2022 Carolyn J. Wild

All rights reserved.

Cover illustration and design by Yulius Gilang Swandika

a roar of laughter that went up to the ceiling of the bank. Since then I bank no more. I keep my money in cash in my trousers pocket and my savings in silver dollars in a sock.

LUCK

by Mark Twain

[Note.—This is not a fancy sketch. I got it from a clergyman who was an instructor at Woolwich forty years ago, and who vouched for its truth.—M. T.]

It was at a banquet in London in honor of one of the two or three conspicuously illustrious English military names of this generation. For reasons which will presently appear, I will withhold his real name and titles, and call him Lieutenant-General Lord Arthur Scoresby, Y.C., K.C.B., etc., etc., etc. What a fascination there is in a renowned name! There sat the man, in actual flesh, whom I had heard of so many thousands of times since that day, thirty years before, when his name shot suddenly to the zenith from a Crimean battlefield, to remain forever celebrated. It was food and drink to me to look, and look, and look at that demigod; scanning, searching, noting: the quietness, the reserve, the noble gravity of his countenance; the simple honesty that expressed itself all over him; the sweet unconsciousness of his greatness—unconsciousness of the hundreds of admiring eyes fastened upon him, unconsciousness of the deep, loving, sincere worship welling out of the breasts of those people and flowing toward him.

The clergyman at my left was an old acquaintance of mine—clergyman now, but had spent the first half of his life in the camp and field, and as an instructor in the military school at Woolwich. Just at the moment I have been talking about, a veiled and singular light glimmered in his eyes, and he leaned down and muttered confidentially to me—indicating the hero of the banquet with a gesture,—

"Privately—he's an absolute fool."

This verdict was a great surprise to me. If its subject had been Napoleon, or Socrates, or Solomon, my astonishment could not have been greater. Two things I was well aware of: that the Reverend was a man of strict veracity, and that his judgment of men was good. Therefore I knew, beyond doubt or question, that the world was mistaken about this hero: he *was* a fool. So I meant to find out, at a convenient moment, how the Reverend, all solitary and alone, had discovered the secret.

Some days later the opportunity came, and this is what the Reverend told me:

About forty years ago I was an instructor in the military academy at Woolwich. I was present in one of the sections when young Scoresby underwent his preliminary examination. I was touched to the quick with pity; for the rest of the class answered up brightly and handsomely, while he—why, dear me, he didn't know *anything*, so to speak. He was evidently good, and sweet, and lovable, and guileless; and so it was exceedingly painful to see him stand there, as serene as a graven image, and deliver himself of answers which were veritably miraculous for stupidity and ignorance. All the compassion in me was aroused in his behalf. I said to myself, when he comes to be examined again, he will be flung over, of course; so it will be simply a harmless act of charity to ease his fall as much as I can. I took him aside, and found that he knew a little of Caesar's history; and as he didn't know anything else, I went to work and drilled him like a galley-slave on a certain line of stock questions concerning Caesar which I knew would be used. If you'll believe me, he went through with flying colors on examination day! He went through on that purely superficial "cram," and got compliments too, while others, who knew a thousand times more than he, got plucked. By some strangely lucky accident—an accident not likely to happen twice in a century—he was asked no question outside of the narrow limits of his drill.

It was stupefying. Well, all through his course I stood by him, with something of the sentiment which a mother feels for a crippled child; and he always saved himself—just by miracle, apparently.

Now of course the thing that would expose him and kill him at last was mathematics. I resolved to make his death as easy as I could; so I drilled him and crammed him, and crammed him and drilled him, just on the line of questions which the examiners would be most likely to use, and then launched him on his fate. Well, sir, try to conceive of the result: to my consternation, he took the first prize! And with it he got a perfect ovation in the way of compliments.

Sleep? There was no more sleep for me for a week. My conscience tortured me day and night. What I had done I had done purely through charity, and only to ease the poor youth's fall—I never had dreamed of any such preposterous result as the thing that had happened. I felt as guilty and miserable as the creator of Frankenstein. Here was a woodenhead whom I had put in the way of glittering promotions and prodigious responsibilities, and but one thing could happen: he and his responsibilities would all go to ruin together at the first opportunity.

The Crimean war had just broken out. Of course there had to be a war, I said to myself: we couldn't have peace and give this donkey a chance to die before he is found out. I waited for the earthquake. It came. And it made me reel when it did come. He was actually gazetted to a captaincy in a marching regiment! Better men grow old and gray in the service before they climb to a sublimity like that. And who could ever have foreseen that they would go and put such a load of responsibility on such green and inadequate shoulders? I could just barely have stood it if they had made him a cornet; but a captain—think of it! I thought my hair would turn white.

Consider what I did—I who so loved repose and inaction. I said to myself, I am responsible to the country for this, and I must go along with him and protect the country against him as far as I can. So I took my poor little capital that I had saved up through years of work and grinding economy, and went with a sigh and bought a cornetcy in his regiment, and away we went to the field.

And there—oh dear, it was awful. Blunders?—why, he never did anything *but* blunder. But, you see, nobody was in the fellow's secret—everybody had him focused wrong, and necessarily misinterpreted his performance every time—consequently they took his idiotic blunders for inspirations of genius; they did, honestly! His mildest blunders were enough to make a man in his right mind cry; and they did make me cry—and rage and rave too, privately. And the thing that kept me always in a sweat of apprehension was the fact that every fresh blunder he made increased the luster of his reputation! I kept saying to myself, he'll get so high, that when discovery does finally come, it will be like the sun falling out of the sky.

He went right along up, from grade to grade, over the dead bodies of his superiors, until at last, in the hottest moment of the battle of **** down went our colonel, and my heart jumped into my mouth, for Scoresby was next in rank! Now for it, said I; we'll all land in Sheol in ten minutes, sure.

The battle was awfully hot; the allies were steadily giving way all over the field. Our regiment occupied a position that was vital; a blunder now must be destruction. At this crucial moment, what does this immortal fool do but detach the regiment from its place and order a charge over a neighboring hill where there wasn't a suggestion of an enemy! "There you go!" I said to myself; "this *is* the end at last."

And away we did go, and were over the shoulder of the hill before the insane movement could be discovered and stopped. And what did we find? An entire and unsuspected Russian army in reserve! And what happened? We were eaten up? That is necessarily what would have happened in ninety-nine cases out of a hundred. But no; those Russians argued that no single regiment would come browsing around there at such a time. It must be the entire English army, and that the sly Russian game was detected and blocked; so they turned tail, and away they went, pell-mell, over the hill and down into the field, in wild confusion, and we after them; they themselves broke the solid Russian center in the field, and tore through, and in no time there was the most tremendous rout you ever saw, and the defeat of the allies was turned into a sweeping and splendid victory! Marshal Canrobert looked on, dizzy with astonishment, admiration, and delight; and sent right off for Scoresby, and hugged him, and decorated him on the field, in presence of all the armies!

And what was Scoresby's blunder that time? Merely the mistaking his right hand for his left—that was all. An order had come to him to fall back and support our right; and instead, he fell *forward* and went over the hill to the left. But the name he won that day as a marvelous military genius filled the world with his glory, and that glory will never fade while history books last.

He is just as good and sweet and lovable and unpretending as a man can be, but he doesn't know enough to come in when it rains. Now that is absolutely true. He is the supremest ass in the universe; and until half an hour ago nobody knew it but himself and me. He has been pursued, day-by-day and year-by-year, by a most phenomenal and astonishing luckiness. He has been a shining soldier in all our wars for a generation; he has littered his whole military life with blunders, and yet has never committed one that didn't make him a knight or a baronet or a lord or something. Look at his breast; why, he is just clothed in domestic and foreign decorations. Well, sir, every one of them is the record of some shouting stupidity or other; and taken together, they are proof that the very best thing in all this world that can befall a man is to be born lucky. I say again, as I said at the banquet, Scoresby's an absolute fool.

THE MOUSE

by Saki

Theodoric Voler had been brought up, from infancy to middle age, by a fond mother whose chief concern had been to keep him screened from what she called the coarser realities of life. When she died she left Theodoric alone in a world that was as real as ever, and a good deal coarser than he considered it had any need to be. To a man of his temperament and upbringing even a simple railway journey was crammed with petty annoyances and minor discords, and as he settled himself down in a second-class compartment one September morning he was conscious of ruffled feelings and general mental discomposure.

He had been staying at a country vicarage, the inmates of which had been certainly neither brutal nor bacchanalian, but their supervision of the domestic establishment had been of that lax order which invites disaster. The pony carriage that was to take him to the station had never been properly ordered, and when the moment for his departure drew near the handyman who should have produced the carriage was nowhere to be found. In this emergency Theodoric, to his mute but very intense disgust, found himself obliged to collaborate with the vicar's daughter in the task of harnessing the pony, which necessitated groping about in an ill-lighted outhouse called a stable, and smelling very like one—except in patches where it smelt of mice. Without being actually afraid of mice, Theodoric classed them among the coarser incidents of life, and considered that Providence, with a little exercise of moral courage, might long ago have recognised that they were not essential, and have withdrawn them from circulation. As the train glided out of the station Theodoric's nervous imagination accused himself of exhaling a weak odour of stable-yard, and possibly of displaying a mouldy straw or two on his usually well-brushed garments.

Fortunately the only other occupant of the compartment, a lady of about the same age as himself, seemed inclined for slumber rather than scrutiny; the train was not due to stop till the terminus was reached, in about an hour's time, and the carriage was of the old-fashioned sort, that held no communication with a corridor, therefore no further travelling companions were likely to intrude on Theodoric's semi-privacy. And yet the train had scarcely attained its normal speed before he became reluctantly but vividly aware that he was not alone with the sleeping lady; he was not even alone in his own clothes.

A warm, creeping movement over his flesh betrayed the unwelcome and highly resented presence, unseen but poignant, of a strayed mouse, that had evidently dashed into its present retreat during the pony harnessing. Furtive stamps and shakes and wildly directed pinches failed to dislodge the intruder; and the lawful occupant of the clothes lay back against the cushions and endeavoured rapidly to think of some means for putting an end to the dual ownership. It was unthinkable that he should continue for the space of a whole hour in the horrible position of a Rowton House for vagrant mice (already his imagination had at least doubled the numbers of the alien invasion). On the other hand, nothing less drastic than partial disrobing would ease him of his tormentor, and to undress in the presence of a lady, even for so laudable a purpose, was an idea that made his ear tips tingle in a blush of abject shame. He had never been able to bring himself even to the mild exposure of open-work socks in the presence of the fair sex. And yet—the lady in this case was to all appearances soundly and securely asleep; the mouse, on the other hand, seemed to be trying to crowd a Wanderjahr into a few strenuous minutes. If there is any truth in the theory of transmigration, this particular mouse must certainly have been in a former state a member of the Alpine Club. Sometimes in its eagerness it lost its footing and slipped for half an inch or so; and then, in fright, or more probably temper, it bit.

Theodoric was goaded into the most audacious undertaking of his life. Crimsoning to the hue of a beetroot and keeping an agonised watch on his slumbering fellow traveller, he swiftly and noiselessly secured the ends of his railway rug to the racks on either side of the carriage, so that a substantial curtain hung across the compartment. In the narrow dressing room that he had improvised he proceeded with violent haste to extricate himself partially and the mouse entirely from the surrounding casings of tweed and half-wool. As the unravelled mouse gave a wild leap to the floor, the rug, slipping its fastening at either end, also came down with a heart-curdling flop, and almost simultaneously the awakened sleeper opened her eyes. With a movement almost quicker than the mouse's, Theodoric pounced on the rug, and hauled its ample folds chin-high over himself as he collapsed into the further corner of the carriage. The blood raced and beat in the veins of his neck and forehead, while he waited dumbly for the communication-cord to be pulled. The lady, however, contented herself with a silent stare at her strangely muffled companion. How much had she seen, Theodoric queried to himself, and in any case what on earth must she think of his present posture?

"I think I have caught a chill," he ventured desperately.

"Really, I'm sorry," she replied. "I was just going to ask you if you would open this window."

"I fancy it's malaria," he added, his teeth chattering slightly, as much from fright as from a desire to support his theory.

"I've got some brandy in my hold-all, if you'll kindly reach it down for me," said his companion.

"Not for worlds—I mean, I never take anything for it," he assured her earnestly.

"I suppose you caught it in the Tropics?"

Theodoric, whose acquaintance with the Tropics was limited to an annual present of a chest of tea from an uncle in Ceylon, felt that even the malaria was slipping from him. Would it be possible, he wondered, to disclose the real state of affairs to her in small instalments?

"Are you afraid of mice?" he ventured, growing, if possible, more scarlet in the face.

"Not unless they came in quantities, like those that ate up Bishop Hatto. Why do you ask?"

"I had one crawling inside my clothes just now," said Theodoric in a voice that hardly seemed his own. "It was a most awkward situation."

"It must have been, if you wear your clothes at all tight," she observed; "but mice have strange ideas of comfort."

"I had to get rid of it while you were asleep," he continued; then, with a gulp, he added, "it was getting rid of it that brought me to—to this."

"Surely leaving off one small mouse wouldn't bring on a chill," she exclaimed, with a levity that Theodoric thought abominable.

Evidently she had detected something of his predicament, and was enjoying his confusion. All the blood in his body seemed to have mobilised in one concentrated blush, and an agony of abasement, worse than a myriad mice, crept up and down over his soul. And then, as reflection began to assert itself, sheer terror took the place of humiliation. With every minute that passed the train was rushing nearer to the crowded and bustling terminus where dozens of prying eyes would be exchanged for the one paralysing pair that watched him from the further corner of the carriage. There was one slender despairing chance, which the next few minutes must decide. His fellow traveller might relapse into a blessed slumber. But as the minutes throbbed by that chance ebbed away. The furtive glance which Theodoric stole at her from time to time disclosed only an unwinking wakefulness.

"I think we must be getting near now," she observed.

Theodoric had already noted with growing terror the recurring stacks of small, ugly dwellings that heralded the journey's end. The words acted as a signal. Like a hunted beast breaking cover and dashing madly towards some other haven of momentary safety he threw aside his rug, and struggled frantically into his dishevelled garments. He was conscious of dull suburban stations racing past the window, of a choking, hammering sensation in his throat and heart, and of an icy silence in that corner towards which he dared not look. Then as he sank back in his seat, clothed and almost delirious, the train slowed down to a final crawl, and the woman spoke.

"Would you be so kind," she asked, "as to get me a porter to put me into a cab? It's a shame to trouble you when you're feeling unwell, but being blind makes one so helpless at a railway station."

HIS LORDSHIP

by W. W. Jacobs

Farmer Rose sat in his porch smoking an evening pipe. By his side, in a comfortable Windsor chair, sat his friend the miller, also smoking, and gazing with half-closed eyes at the landscape as he listened for the thousandth time to his host's complaints about his daughter.

"The long and the short of it is, Cray," said the farmer, with an air of mournful pride, "she's far too good-looking."

Mr. Cray grunted.

"Truth is truth, though she's my daughter," continued Mr. Rose, vaguely. "She's too good-looking. Sometimes when I've taken her up to market I've seen the folks fair turn their backs on the cattle and stare at her instead."

Mr. Cray sniffed; louder, perhaps, than he had intended. "Beautiful that rosebush smells," he remarked, as his friend turned and eyed him.

"What is the consequence?" demanded the farmer, relaxing his gaze. "She looks in the glass and sees herself, and then she gets miserable and uppish because there ain't nobody in these parts good enough for her to marry."

"It's a extraordinary thing to me where she gets them good looks from," said the miller, deliberately.

"Ah!" said Mr. Rose, and sat trying to think of a means of enlightening his friend without undue loss of modesty.

"She ain't a bit like her poor mother," mused Mr. Cray.

"No, she don't get her looks from her," assented the other.

"It's one o' them things you can't account for," said Mr. Cray, who was very tired of the subject; "it's just like seeing a beautiful flower blooming on an old cabbage-stump."

The farmer knocked his pipe out noisily and began to refill it. "People have said that she takes after me a trifle," he remarked, shortly.

"You weren't fool enough to believe that, I know," said the miller. "Why, she's no more like you than you're like a warming-pan—not so much."

Mr. Rose regarded his friend fixedly. "You ain't got a very nice way o' putting things, Cray," he said, mournfully.

"I'm no flatterer," said the miller; "never was, and you can't please everybody. If I said your daughter took after you I don't s'pose she'd ever speak to me again."

"The worst of it is," said the farmer, disregarding his remark, "she won't settle down. There's young Walter Lomas after her now, and she won't look at him. He's a decent young fellow is Walter, and she's been and named one o' the pigs after him, and the way she mixes them up together is disgraceful."

"If she was my girl she should marry young Walter," said the miller, firmly. "What's wrong with him?"

"She looks higher," replied the other, mysteriously; "she's always reading them romantic books full o' love tales, and she's never tired o' talking of a girl her mother used to know that went on the stage and married a baronet. She goes and sits in the best parlour every afternoon now, and calls it the drawing room. She'll sit there till she's past the marrying age, and then she'll turn round and blame me."

"She wants a lesson," said Mr. Cray, firmly. "She wants to be taught her position in life, not to go about turning up her nose at young men and naming pigs after them."

"What she wants to understand is that the upper classes wouldn't look at her," pursued the miller.

"It would be easier to make her understand that if they didn't," said the farmer.

"I mean," said Mr. Cray, sternly, "with a view to marriage. What you ought to do is to get somebody staying down here with you pretending to be a lord or a nobleman, and ordering her about and not noticing her good looks at all. Then, while she's upset about that, in comes Walter Lomas to comfort her and be a contrast to the other."

Mr. Rose withdrew his pipe and regarded him open-mouthed.

"Yes; but how—" he began.

"And it seems to me," interrupted Mr. Cray, "that I know just the young fellow to do it—nephew of my wife's.

He was coming to stay a fortnight with us, but you can have him with pleasure—me and him don't get on over and above well."

"Perhaps he wouldn't do it," objected the farmer.

"He'd do it like a shot," said Mr. Cray, positively. "It would be fun for us and it 'ud be a lesson for her. If you like, I'll tell him to write to you for lodgings, as he wants to come for a fortnight's fresh air after the fatiguing amusements of town."

"Fatiguing amusements of town," repeated the admiring farmer. "Fatiguing—"

He sat back in his chair and laughed, and Mr. Cray, delighted at the prospect of getting rid so easily of a tiresome guest, laughed too. Overhead at the open window a third person laughed, but in so quiet and well-bred a fashion that neither of them heard her.

The farmer received a letter a day or two afterwards, and negotiations between Jane Rose on the one side and Lord Fairmount on the other were soon in progress; the farmer's own composition being deemed somewhat crude for such a correspondence.

"I wish he didn't want it kept so secret," said Miss Rose, pondering over the final letter. "I should like to let the Crays and one or two more people know he is staying with us. However, I suppose he must have his own way."

"You must do as he wishes," said her father, using his handkerchief violently.

Jane sighed. "He'll be a little company for me, at any rate," she remarked. "What is the matter, father?"

"Bit of a cold," said the farmer, indistinctly, as he made

for the door, still holding his handkerchief to his face. "Been coming on some time."

He put on his hat and went out, and Miss Rose, watching him from the window, was not without fears that the joke might prove too much for a man of his habit. She regarded him thoughtfully, and when he returned at one o'clock to dinner, and encountered instead a violent dust storm which was raging in the house, she noted with pleasure that his sense of humour was more under control.

"Dinner?" she said, as he strove to squeeze past the furniture which was piled in the hall. "We've got no time to think of dinner, and if we had there's no place for you to eat it. You'd better go in the larder and cut yourself a crust of bread and cheese."

Her father hesitated and glared at the servant, who, with her head bound up in a duster, passed at the double with a broom. Then he walked slowly into the kitchen.

Miss Rose called out something after him.

"Eh?" said her father, coming back hopefully.

"How is your cold, dear?"

The farmer made no reply, and his daughter smiled contentedly as she heard him stamping about in the larder. He made but a poor meal, and then, refusing point-blank to assist Annie in moving the piano, went and smoked a very reflective pipe in the garden.

Lord Fairmount arrived the following day on foot from the station, and after acknowledging the farmer's salute with a distant nod requested him to send a cart for his luggage. He was a tall, good-looking young man, and as he stood in the hall languidly twisting his moustache Miss

Rose deliberately decided upon his destruction.

"These your daughters?" he inquired, carelessly, as he followed his host into the parlour.

"One of 'em is, my lord; the other is my servant," replied the farmer.

"She's got your eyes," said his lordship, tapping the astonished Annie under the chin; "your nose too, I think."

"That's my servant," said the farmer, knitting his brows at him.

"Oh, indeed!" said his lordship, airily.

He turned round and regarded Jane, but, although she tried to meet him halfway by elevating her chin a little, his audacity failed him and the words died away on his tongue. A long silence followed, broken only by the ill-suppressed giggles of Annie, who had retired to the kitchen.

"I trust that we shall make your lordship comfortable," said Miss Rose.

"I hope so, my good girl," was the reply. "And now will you show me my room?"

Miss Rose led the way upstairs and threw open the door; Lord Fairmount, pausing on the threshold, gazed at it disparagingly.

"Is this the best room you have?" he inquired, stiffly.

"Oh, no," said Miss Rose, smiling; "father's room is much better than this. Look here."

She threw open another door and, ignoring a gesticulating figure which stood in the hall below, regarded him anxiously. "If you would prefer father's room he would be delighted for you to have it. Delighted."

"Yes, I will have this one," said Lord Fairmount, entering. "Bring me up some hot water, please, and clear these boots and leggings out."

Miss Rose tripped downstairs and, bestowing a witching smile upon her sire, waved away his request for an explanation and hastened into the kitchen, where Annie shortly afterwards emerged with the water.

It was with something of a shock that the farmer discovered that he had to wait for his dinner while his lordship had luncheon. That meal, under his daughter's management, took a long time, and the joint when it reached him was more than half cold. It was, moreover, quite clear that the aristocracy had not even mastered the rudiments of carving, but preferred instead to box the compass for tit-bits.

He ate his meal in silence, and when it was over sought out his guest to administer a few much-needed stage directions. Owing, however, to the ubiquity of Jane he wasted nearly the whole of the afternoon before he obtained an opportunity. Even then the interview was short, the farmer having to compress into ten seconds instructions for Lord Fairmount to express a desire to take his meals with the family, and his dinner at the respectable hour of 1 p.m. Instructions as to a change of bedroom were frustrated by the reappearance of Jane.

His lordship went for a walk after that, and coming back with a bored air stood on the hearthrug in the living room and watched Miss Rose sewing.

"Very dull place," he said at last, in a dissatisfied voice.

"Yes, my lord," said Miss Rose, demurely.

"Fearfully dull," complained his lordship, stifling a yawn. "What I'm to do to amuse myself for a fortnight I'm sure I don't know."

Miss Rose raised her fine eyes and regarded him intently. Many a lesser man would have looked no farther for amusement.

"I'm afraid there is not much to do about here, my lord," she said quietly. "We are very plain folk in these parts."

"Yes," assented the other. An obvious compliment rose of itself to his lips, but he restrained himself, though with difficulty. Miss Rose bent her head over her work and stitched industriously. His lordship took up a book and, remembering his mission, read for a couple of hours without taking the slightest notice of her. Miss Rose glanced over in his direction once or twice, and then, with a somewhat vixenish expression on her delicate features, resumed her sewing.

"Wonderful eyes she's got," said the gentleman, as he sat on the edge of his bed that night and thought over the events of the day. "It's pretty to see them flash."

He saw them flash several times during the next few days, and Mr. Rose himself, was more than satisfied with the hauteur with which his guest treated the household.

"But I don't like the way you have with me," he complained.

"It's all in the part," urged his lordship.

"Well, you can leave that part out," replied Mr. Rose, with some acerbity. "I object to being spoke to as you speak to me before that girl Annie. Be as proud and unpleasant as you like to my daughter, but leave me alone. Mind that!"

His lordship promised, and in pursuance of his host's instructions strove manfully to subdue feelings towards Miss Rose by no means in accordance with them. The best of us are liable to absent-mindedness, and he sometimes so far forgot himself as to address her in tones as humble as any in her somewhat large experience.

"I hope that we are making you comfortable here, my lord?" she said, as they sat together one afternoon.

"I have never been more comfortable in my life," was the gracious reply.

Miss Rose shook her head. "Oh, my lord," she said, in protest, "think of your mansion."

His lordship thought of it. For two or three days he had been thinking of houses and furniture and other things of that nature.

"I have never seen an old country seat," continued Miss Rose, clasping her hands and gazing at him wistfully. "I should be so grateful if your lordship would describe yours to me."

His lordship shifted uneasily, and then, in face of the girl's persistence, stood for some time divided between the contending claims of Hampton Court Palace and the Tower of London. He finally decided upon the former, after first refurnishing it at Maple's.

"How happy you must be!" said the breathless Jane, when he had finished.

He shook his head gravely. "My possessions have never given me any happiness," he remarked. "I would much rather be in a humble rank of life. Live where I like, and—and marry whom I like."

There was no mistaking the meaning fall in his voice. Miss Rose sighed gently and lowered her eyes—her lashes had often excited comment. Then, in a soft voice, she asked him the sort of life he would prefer.

In reply, his lordship, with an eloquence which surprised himself, portrayed the joys of life in a seven-roomed house in town, with a greenhouse six feet by three, and a garden large enough to contain it. He really spoke well, and when he had finished his listener gazed at him with eyes suffused with timid admiration.

"Oh, my lord," she said, prettily, "now I know what you've been doing. You've been slumming."

"Slumming?" gasped his lordship.

"You couldn't have described a place like that unless you had been," said Miss Rose nodding. "I hope you took the poor people some nice hot soup."

His lordship tried to explain, but without success. Miss Rose persisted in regarding him as a missionary of food and warmth, and spoke feelingly of the people who had to live in such places. She also warned him against the risk of infection.

"You don't understand," he repeated, impatiently. "These are nice houses—nice enough for anybody to live in. If you took soup to people like that, why, they'd throw it at you."

"Wretches!" murmured the indignant Jane, who was enjoying herself amazingly.

His lordship eyed her with sudden suspicion, but her face was quite grave and bore traces of strong feeling. He explained again, but without avail.

"You never ought to go near such places, my lord," she concluded, solemnly, as she rose to quit the room. "Even a girl of my station would draw the line at that."

She bowed deeply and withdrew. His lordship sank into a chair and, thrusting his hands into his pockets, gazed gloomily at the dried grasses in the grate.

During the next day or two his appetite failed, and other well-known symptoms set in. Miss Rose, diagnosing them all, prescribed by stealth some bitter remedies. The farmer regarded his change of manner with disapproval, and, concluding that it was due to his own complaints, sought to reassure him. He also pointed out that his daughter's opinion of the aristocracy was hardly likely to increase if the only member she knew went about the house as though he had just lost his grandmother.

"You are longing for the amusements of town, my lord," he remarked one morning at breakfast.

His lordship shook his head. The amusements comprised, amongst other things, a stool and a desk.

"I don't like town," he said, with a glance at Jane. "If I had my choice I would live here always. I would sooner live here in this charming spot with this charming society than anywhere."

Mr. Rose coughed and, having caught his eye, shook his head at him and glanced significantly over at the unconscious Jane. The young man ignored his action and, having got an opening, gave utterance in the course of the next ten minutes to Radical heresies of so violent a type that the farmer could hardly keep his seat. Social distinctions were condemned utterly, and the House of

Lords referred to as a human dustbin. The farmer gazed open-mouthed at this snake he had nourished.

"Your lordship will alter your mind when you get to town," said Jane, demurely.

"Never!" declared the other, impressively.

The girl sighed, and gazing first with much interest at her parent, who seemed to be doing his best to ward off a fit, turned her lustrous eyes upon the guest.

"We shall all miss you," she said, softly. "You've been a lesson to all of us."

"Lesson?" he repeated, flushing.

"It has improved our behaviour so, having a lord in the house," said Miss Rose, with painful humility. "I'm sure father hasn't been like the same man since you've been here."

"What d'ye mean Miss?" demanded the farmer, hotly.

"Don't speak like that before his lordship, father," said his daughter, hastily. "I'm not blaming you; you're no worse than the other men about here. You haven't had an opportunity of learning before, that's all. It isn't your fault."

"Learning?" bellowed the farmer, turning an inflamed visage upon his apprehensive guest. "Have you noticed anything wrong about my behaviour?"

"Certainly not," said his lordship, hastily.

"All I know is," continued Miss Rose, positively, "I wish you were going to stay here another six months for father's sake."

"Look here—" began Mr. Rose, smiting the table.

"And Annie's," said Jane, raising her voice above the

din. "I don't know which has improved the most. I'm sure the way they both drink their tea now—"

Mr. Rose pushed his chair back loudly and got up from the table. For a moment he stood struggling for words, then he turned suddenly with a growl and quitted the room, banging the door after him in a fashion which clearly indicated that he still had some lessons to learn.

"You've made your father angry," said his lordship.

"It's for his own good," said Miss Rose. "Are you really sorry to leave us?"

"Sorry?" repeated the other. "Sorry is no word for it."

"You will miss father," said the girl.

He sighed gently.

"And Annie," she continued.

He sighed again, and Jane took a slight glance at him cornerwise.

"And me too, I hope," she said, in a low voice.

"Miss you!" repeated his lordship, in a suffocating voice. "I should miss the sun less."

"I am so glad," said Jane, clasping her hands; "it is so nice to feel that one is not quite forgotten. Of course, I can never forget you. You are the only nobleman I have ever met."

"I hope that it is not only because of that," he said, forlornly.

Miss Rose pondered. When she pondered her eyes increased in size and revealed unsuspected depths.

"No-o," she said at length, in a hesitating voice.

"Suppose that I were not what I am represented to be," he said slowly. "Suppose that, instead of being Lord

Fairmount, I were merely a clerk."

"A clerk?" repeated Miss Rose, with a very well-managed shudder. "How can I suppose such an absurd thing as that?"

"But if I were?" urged his lordship, feverishly.

"It's no use supposing such a thing as that," said Miss Rose, briskly; "your high birth is stamped on you."

His lordship shook his head.

"I would sooner be a labourer on this farm than a king anywhere else," he said, with feeling.

Miss Rose drew a pattern on the floor with the toe of her shoe.

"The poorest labourer on the farm can have the pleasure of looking at you every day," continued his lordship passionately. "Every day of his life he can see you, and feel a better man for it."

Miss Rose looked at him sharply. Only the day before the poorest labourer had seen her—when he wasn't expecting the honour—and received an epitome of his character which had nearly stunned him. But his lordship's face was quite grave.

"I go tomorrow," he said.

"Yes," said Jane, in a hushed voice.

He crossed the room gently and took a seat by her side. Miss Rose, still gazing at the floor, wondered indignantly why it was she was not blushing. His Lordship's conversation had come to a sudden stop and the silence was most awkward.

"I've been a fool, Miss Rose," he said at last, rising and standing over her; "and I've been taking a great liberty. I've been deceiving you for nearly a fortnight."

"Nonsense!" responded Miss Rose, briskly.

"I have been deceiving you," he repeated. "I have made you believe that I am a person of title."

"Nonsense!" said Miss Rose again.

The other started and eyed her uneasily.

"Nobody would mistake you for a lord," said Miss Rose, cruelly. "Why, I shouldn't think that you had ever seen one. You didn't do it at all properly. Why, your uncle Cray would have done it better."

Mr. Cray's nephew fell back in consternation and eyed her dumbly as she laughed. All mirth is not contagious, and he was easily able to refrain from joining in this.

"I can't understand," said Miss Rose as she wiped a tear-dimmed eye—"I can't understand how you could have thought I should be so stupid."

"I've been a fool," said the other, bitterly, as he retreated to the door. "Goodbye."

"Goodbye," said Jane. She looked him full in the face, and the blushes for which she had been waiting came in force. "You needn't go, unless you want to," she said, softly. "I like fools better than lords."

HOODOO MCFIGGIN'S CHRISTMAS

by Stephen Leacock

This Santa Claus business is played out. It's a sneaking, underhand method, and the sooner it's exposed the better.

For a parent to get up under cover of the darkness of night and palm off a ten-cent necktie on a boy who had been expecting a ten-dollar watch, and then say that an angel sent it to him, is low, undeniably low.

I had a good opportunity of observing how the thing worked this Christmas, in the case of young Hoodoo McFiggin, the son and heir of the McFiggins, at whose house I board.

Hoodoo McFiggin is a good boy—a religious boy. He had been given to understand that Santa Claus would bring nothing to his father and mother because grown-up people don't get presents from the angels. So he saved up all his pocket money and bought a box of cigars for his father and a seventy-five-cent diamond brooch for his mother. His own fortunes he left in the hands of the angels. But he prayed. He prayed every night for weeks that Santa Claus would bring him a pair of skates and a puppy dog and an air-gun and a bicycle and a Noah's ark and a sleigh and a drum—altogether about a hundred and fifty dollars' worth of stuff.

I went into Hoodoo's room quite early Christmas morning. I had an idea that the scene would be interesting. I woke him up and he sat up in bed, his eyes glistening with radiant expectation, and began hauling things out of his stocking.

The first parcel was bulky; it was done up quite loosely and had an odd look generally.

"Ha! Ha!" Hoodoo cried gleefully, as he began undoing it. "I'll bet it's the puppy dog, all wrapped up in paper!"

And was it the puppy dog? No, by no means. It was a pair of nice, strong, number-four boots, laces and all, labelled, "Hoodoo, from Santa Claus," and underneath Santa Claus had written, "95 net."

The boy's jaw fell with delight. "It's boots," he said, and plunged in his hand again.

He began hauling away at another parcel with renewed hope on his face.

This time the thing seemed like a little round box. Hoodoo tore the paper off it with a feverish hand. He shook it; something rattled inside.

"It's a watch and chain! It's a watch and chain!" he shouted. Then he pulled the lid off.

And was it a watch and chain? No. It was a box of nice,

brand-new celluloid collars, a dozen of them all alike and all his own size.

The boy was so pleased that you could see his face crack up with pleasure.

He waited a few minutes until his intense joy subsided. Then he tried again.

This time the packet was long and hard. It resisted the touch and had a sort of funnel shape.

"It's a toy pistol!" said the boy, trembling with excitement. "Gee! I hope there are lots of caps with it! I'll fire some off now and wake up father."

No, my poor child, you will not wake your father with that. It is a useful thing, but it needs not caps and it fires no bullets, and you cannot wake a sleeping man with a toothbrush. Yes, it was a toothbrush—a regular beauty, pure bone all through, and ticketed with a little paper, "Hoodoo, from Santa Claus."

Again the expression of intense joy passed over the boy's face, and the tears of gratitude started from his eyes. He wiped them away with his toothbrush and passed on.

The next packet was much larger and evidently contained something soft and bulky. It had been too long to go into the stocking and was tied outside.

"I wonder what this is," Hoodoo mused, half afraid to open it. Then his heart gave a great leap, and he forgot all his other presents in the anticipation of this one. "It's the drum!" he gasped. "It's the drum, all wrapped up!"

Drum nothing! It was pants—a pair of the nicest little short pants—yellowish-brown short pants—with dear little stripes of colour running across both ways, and here again Santa Claus had written, "Hoodoo, from Santa Claus, one fort net."

But there was something wrapped up in it. Oh, yes! There was a pair of braces wrapped up in it, braces with a little steel sliding thing so that you could slide your pants up to your neck, if you wanted to.

The boy gave a dry sob of satisfaction. Then he took out his last present. "It's a book," he said, as he unwrapped it. "I wonder if it is fairy stories or adventures. Oh, I hope it's adventures! I'll read it all morning."

No, Hoodoo, it was not precisely adventures. It was a small family Bible. Hoodoo had now seen all his presents, and he arose and dressed. But he still had the fun of playing with his toys. That is always the chief delight of Christmas morning.

First he played with his toothbrush. He got a whole lot of water and brushed all his teeth with it. This was huge.

Then he played with his collars. He had no end of fun with them, taking them all out one by one and swearing at them, and then putting them back and swearing at the whole lot together.

The next toy was his pants. He had immense fun there, putting them on and taking them off again, and then trying to guess which side was which by merely looking at them.

After that he took his book and read some adventures called "Genesis" till breakfast-time.

Then he went downstairs and kissed his father and mother. His father was smoking a cigar, and his mother had her new brooch on. Hoodoo's face was thoughtful, and a light seemed to have broken in upon his mind. Indeed, I think it altogether likely that next Christmas he will hang on to his own money and take chances on what the angels bring.

THE INCONSIDERATE WAITER

by J. M. Barrie

Frequently I have to ask myself in the street for the name of the man I bowed to just now, and then, before I can answer, the wind of the first corner blows him from my memory. I have a theory, however, that those puzzling faces, which pass before I can see who cut the coat, all belong to club waiters.

Until William forced his affairs upon me that was all I did know of the private life of waiters, though I have been in the club for twenty years. I was even unaware whether they slept downstairs or had their own homes; nor had I the interest to inquire of other members, nor they the knowledge to inform me. I hold that this sort of people should be fed and clothed and given airing and wives and children, and I subscribe yearly, I believe for these purposes; but to come into closer relation with waiters is bad form; they are club fittings, and William should have kept his distress to himself, or taken it away and patched it up like a rent in one of the chairs. His inconsiderateness has been a pair of spectacles to me for months.

It is not correct taste to know the name of a club waiter, so I must apologise for knowing William's, and still more for not forgetting it. If, again, to speak of a waiter is bad form, to speak bitterly is the comic degree of it. But William has disappointed me sorely. There were years when I would defer dining several minutes that he might wait on me. His pains to reserve the window seat for me were perfectly satisfactory. I allowed him privileges, as to suggest dishes, and would give him information, as that someone had startled me in the reading room by slamming a door. I have shown him how I cut my finger with a piece of string. Obviously he was gratified by these attentions, usually recommending a liqueur; and I fancy he must have understood my sufferings, for he often looked ill himself. Probably he was rheumatic, but I cannot say for certain, as I never thought of asking, and he had the sense to see that the knowledge would be offensive to me.

In the smoking room we have a waiter so independent that once, when he brought me a yellow chartreuse, and I said I had ordered green, he replied, "No, sir; you said yellow." William could never have been guilty of such effrontery. In appearance, of course, he is mean, but I can no more describe him than a milkmaid could draw cows. I suppose we distinguish one waiter from another much as we pick our hat from the rack. We could have plotted a murder safely before William. He never presumed to have any opinions of his own. When such was my mood he remained silent, and if I announced that something diverting had happened to me he laughed before I told him what it was. He turned the twinkle in his eye off or on at my bidding as readily as if it was the gas. To my "Sure to be wet tomorrow," he would reply, "Yes, sir;" and to Trelawney's "It doesn't look like rain," two minutes afterward, he would reply, "No, sir." It was one member who said Lightning Rod would win the Derby and another who said Lightning Rod had no chance, but it was William who agreed with both. He was like a cheroot, which may be smoked from either end. So used was I to him that, had he died or got another situation (or whatever it is such persons do when they disappear from the club), I should probably have told the head waiter to bring him back, as I disliked changes.

It would not become me to know precisely when I began to think William an ingrate, but I date his lapse from the evening when he brought me oysters. I detest oysters, and no one knew it better than William. He has agreed with me that he could not understand any gentleman's liking them. Between me and a certain member who smacks his lips twelve times to a dozen of them William knew I liked a screen to be placed until we had reached the soup, and yet he gave me the oysters and the other man my sardine. Both the other member and I quickly called for brandy and the head waiter. To do William justice, he shook, but never can I forget his audacious explanation: "Beg pardon, sir, but I was thinking of something else."

In these words William had flung off the mask, and

now I knew him for what he was.

I must not be accused of bad form for looking at William on the following evening. What prompted me to do so was not personal interest in him, but a desire to see whether I dare let him wait on me again. So, recalling that a caster was off a chair yesterday, one is entitled to make sure that it is on today before sitting down. If the expression is not too strong, I may say that I was taken aback by William's manner. Even when crossing the room to take my orders he let his one hand play nervously with the other. I had to repeat "Sardine on toast" twice, and instead of answering, "Yes, sir," as if my selection of sardine on toast was a personal gratification to him, which is the manner one expects of a waiter, he glanced at the clock, then out at the window, and, starting, asked, "Did you say sardine on toast, sir?"

It was the height of summer, when London smells like a chemist's shop, and he who has the dinner table at the window needs no candles to show him his knife and fork. I lay back at intervals, now watching a starved-looking woman sleep on a doorstep, and again complaining of the club bananas. By-and-by I saw a girl of the commonest kind, ill-clad and dirty. Parents should be compelled to feed and clothe children comfortably, or at least to keep them indoors, where they cannot offend our eyes. Such children are for pushing aside with one's umbrella; but this girl I noticed because she was gazing at the club windows. She had stood thus for perhaps ten minutes when I became aware that someone was leaning over me to look out at the window. I turned round. Conceive my indignation on seeing that the rude person was William.

"How dare you, William?" I said, sternly. He seemed not to hear me. Let me tell, in the measured words of one describing a past incident, what then took place. To get nearer the window he pressed heavily on my shoulder.

"William, you forget yourself!" I said, meaning—as I see now—that he had forgotten me.

I heard him gulp, but not to my reprimand. He was scanning the street. His hands chattered on my shoulder, and, pushing him from me, I saw that his mouth was agape.

"What are you looking for?" I asked.

He stared at me, and then, like one who had at last heard the echo of my question, seemed to be brought back to the club. He turned his face from me for an instant, and answered shakily:

"I beg your pardon, sir! I—I shouldn't have done it. Are the bananas too ripe, sir?"

He recommended the nuts, and awaited my verdict so anxiously while I ate one that I was about to speak graciously, when I again saw his eyes drag him to the window.

"William," I said, my patience giving way at last, "I dislike being waited on by a melancholy waiter."

"Yes, sir," he replied, trying to smile, and then broke out passionately, "For God's sake, sir, tell me, have you seen a little girl looking in at the club windows?"

He had been a good waiter once, and his distracted visage was spoiling my dinner.

"There," I said, pointing to the girl, and no doubt would

have added that he must bring me coffee immediately, had he continued to listen. But already he was beckoning to the child. I have not the least interest in her (indeed, it had never struck me that waiters had private affairs, and I still think it a pity that they should have); but as I happened to be looking out at the window I could not avoid seeing what occurred. As soon as the girl saw William she ran into the street, regardless of vehicles, and nodded three times to him. Then she disappeared.

I have said that she was quite a common child, without attraction of any sort, and yet it was amazing the difference she made in William. He gasped relief, like one who had broken through the anxiety that checks breathing, and into his face there came a silly laugh of happiness. I had dined well, on the whole, so I said:

"I am glad to see you cheerful again, William."

I meant that I approved his cheerfulness because it helped my digestion, but he must have thought I was sympathising with him.

"Thank you, sir," he answered. "Oh, sir! When she nodded and I saw it was all right I could have gone down on my knees to God."

I was as much horrified as if he had dropped a plate on my toes. Even William, disgracefully emotional as he was at the moment, flung out his arms to recall the shameful words.

"Coffee, William!" I said, sharply.

I sipped my coffee indignantly, for it was plain to me that William had something on his mind.

"You are not vexed with me, sir?" he had the boldness

to whisper.

"It was a liberty," I said.

"I know, sir; but I was beside myself."

"That was a liberty also."

He hesitated, and then blurted out:

"It is my wife, sir. She—"

I stopped him with my hand. William, whom I had favoured in so many ways, was a married man! I might have guessed as much years before had I ever reflected about waiters, for I knew vaguely that his class did this sort of thing. His confession was distasteful to me, and I said warningly:

"Remember where you are, William."

"Yes, sir; but you see, she is so delicate—"

"Delicate! I forbid your speaking to me on unpleasant topics."

"Yes, sir; begging your pardon."

It was characteristic of William to beg my pardon and withdraw his wife, like some unsuccessful dish, as if its taste would not remain in the mouth. I shall be chided for questioning him further about his wife, but, though doubtless an unusual step, it was only bad form superficially, for my motive was irreproachable. I inquired for his wife, not because I was interested in her welfare, but in the hope of allaying my irritation. So I am entitled to invite the wayfarer who has bespattered me with mud to scrape it off.

I desired to be told by William that the girl's signals meant his wife's recovery to health. He should have seen that such was my wish and answered accordingly. But, with the brutal inconsiderateness of his class, he said:

"She has had a good day; but the doctor, he—the doctor is afraid she is dying."

Already I repented my questions. William and his wife seemed in league against me, when they might so easily have chosen some other member.

"Pooh, the doctor!" I said.

"Yes, sir," he answered.

"Have you been married long, William?"

"Eight years, sir. Eight years ago she was—I—I mind her when . . . and now the doctor says—"

The fellow gaped at me. "More coffee, sir?" he asked.

"What is her ailment?"

"She was always one of the delicate kind, but full of spirit, and—and you see, she has had a baby lately—"

"William!"

"And she—I—the doctor is afraid she's not picking up."

"I feel sure she will pick up."

"Yes, sir?"

It must have been the wine I had drunk that made me tell him:

"I was once married, William. My wife—it was just such a case as yours."

"She did not get better sir?"

"No."

After a pause he said, "Thank you, sir," meaning for the sympathy that made me tell him that. But it must have been the wine.

"That little girl comes here with a message from your wife?"

"Yes; if she nods three times it means my wife is a little better."

"She nodded thrice today."

"But she is told to do that to relieve me, and maybe those nods don't tell the truth."

"Is she your girl?"

"No; we have none but the baby. She is a neighbour's; she comes twice a day."

"It is heartless of her parents not to send her every hour."

"But she is six years old," he said, "and has a house and two sisters to look after in the daytime, and a dinner to cook. Gentlefolk don't understand."

"I suppose you live in some low part, William."

"Off Drury Lane," he answered, flushing; "but—but it isn't low. You see, we were never used to anything better, and I mind when I let her see the house before we were married, she—she sort of cried because she was so proud of it. That was eight years ago, and now—she's afraid she'll die when I'm away at my work."

"Did she tell you that?"

"Never; she always says she is feeling a little stronger."

"Then how can you know she is afraid of that?"

"I don't know how I know, sir; but when I am leaving the house in the morning I look at her from the door, and she looks at me, and then I—I know."

"A green chartreuse, William!"

I tried to forget William's vulgar story in billiards, but he had spoiled my game. My opponent, to whom I can give twenty, ran out when I was sixty-seven, and I put aside my cue pettishly. That in itself was bad form, but what would they have thought had they known that a waiter's impertinence caused it! I grew angrier with William as the night wore on, and next day I punished him by giving my orders through another waiter.

As I had my window seat, I could not but see that the girl was late again. Somehow I dawdled over my coffee. I had an evening paper before me, but there was so little in it that my eyes found more of interest in the street. It did not matter to me whether William's wife died, but when that girl had promised to come, why did she not come? These lower classes only give their word to break it. The coffee was undrinkable.

At last I saw her. William was at another window, pretending to do something with the curtains. I stood up, pressing closer to the window. The coffee had been so bad that I felt shaky. She nodded three times, and smiled.

"She is a little better," William whispered to me, almost happily.

"Whom are you speaking of?" I asked, coldly, and immediately retired to the billiard room, where I played a capital game. The coffee was much better there than in the dining room.

Several days passed, and I took care to show William that I had forgotten his maunderings. I chanced to see the little girl (though I never looked for her) every evening, and she always nodded three times, save once, when she shook her head, and then William's face grew white as a napkin. I remember this incident because that night I could not get into a pocket. So badly did I play that the thought of it kept me awake in bed, and that, again, made me wonder how William's wife was. Next day I went to the club early (which was not my custom) to see the new books. Being in the club at any rate, I looked into the dining room to ask William if I had left my gloves there, and the sight of him reminded me of his wife; so I asked for her. He shook his head mournfully, and I went off in a rage.

So accustomed am I to the club that when I dine elsewhere I feel uncomfortable next morning, as if I had missed a dinner. William knew this; yet here he was, hounding me out of the club! That evening I dined (as the saying is) at a restaurant, where no sauce was served with the asparagus. Furthermore, as if that were not triumph enough for William, his doleful face came between me and every dish, and I seemed to see his wife dying to annoy me.

I dined next day at the club for self-preservation, taking, however, a table in the middle of the room, and engaging a waiter who had once nearly poisoned me by not interfering when I put two lumps of sugar into my coffee instead of one, which is my allowance. But no William came to me to acknowledge his humiliation, and by-and-by I became aware that he was not in the room. Suddenly the thought struck me that his wife must be dead, and I— It was the worst cooked and the worst served dinner I ever had in the club.

I tried the smoking room. Usually the talk there is entertaining, but on that occasion it was so frivolous that I did not remain five minutes. In the card room a member told me excitedly that a policeman had spoken rudely to him; and my strange comment was:

"After all, it is a small matter."

In the library, where I had not been for years, I found two members asleep, and, to my surprise, William on a ladder dusting books.

"You have not heard, sir?" he said, in answer to my raised eyebrows. Descending the ladder, he whispered tragically: "It was last evening, sir. I—I lost my head, and I—swore at a member."

I stepped back from William, and glanced apprehensively at the two members. They still slept.

"I hardly knew," William went on, "what I was doing all day yesterday, for I had left my wife so weakly that—"

I stamped my foot.

"I beg your pardon for speaking of her," he had the grace to say, "but I couldn't help slipping up to the window often yesterday to look for Jenny, and when she did come, and I saw she was crying, it—it sort of confused me, and I didn't know right, sir, what I was doing. I brushed against a member, Mr. Myddleton Finch, and he—he jumped and swore at me. Well, sir, I had just touched him after all, and I was so miserable, it a kind of stung me to be treated like—like that, and me a man as well as him; and I lost my senses, and—and I swore back."

William's shamed head sank on his chest, but I even let pass his insolence in likening himself to a member of the club, so afraid was I of the sleepers waking and detecting me in talk with a waiter.

"For the love of God," William cried, with coarse emotion, "don't let them dismiss me!"

"Speak lower!" I said. "Who sent you here?"

"I was turned out of the dining room at once, and told to attend to the library until they had decided what to do with me. Oh, sir, I'll lose my place!"

He was blubbering, as if a change of waiters was a matter of importance.

"This is very bad, William," I said. "I fear I can do nothing for you."

"Have mercy on a distracted man!" he entreated. "I'll go on my knees to Mr. Myddleton Finch."

How could I but despise a fellow who would be thus abject for a pound a week?

"I dare not tell her," he continued, "that I have lost my place. She would just fall back and die."

"I forbade your speaking of your wife," I said, sharply, "unless you can speak pleasantly of her."

"But she may be worse now, sir, and I cannot even see Jenny from here. The library windows look to the back."

"If she dies," I said, "it will be a warning to you to marry a stronger woman next time."

Now everyone knows that there is little real affection among the lower orders. As soon as they have lost one mate they take another. Yet William, forgetting our relative positions, drew himself up and raised his fist, and if I had not stepped back I swear he would have struck me.

The highly improper words William used I will omit, out of consideration for him. Even while he was apologising for them I retired to the smoking room, where I found the cigarettes so badly rolled that they would not keep alight. After a little I remembered that I wanted to see Myddleton Finch about an improved saddle of which a friend of his has the patent. He was in the newsroom, and, having questioned him about the saddle, I said:

"By the way, what is this story about your swearing at one of the waiters?"

"You mean about his swearing at me," Myddleton Finch replied, reddening.

"I am glad that was it," I said; "for I could not believe you guilty of such bad form."

"If I did swear—" he was beginning, but I went on:

"The version which has reached me was that you swore at him, and he repeated the word. I heard he was to be dismissed and you reprimanded."

"Who told you that?" asked Myddleton Finch, who is a timid man.

"I forget; it is club talk," I replied, lightly. "But of course the committee will take your word. The waiter, whichever one he is, richly deserves his dismissal for insulting you without provocation."

Then our talk returned to the saddle, but Myddleton Finch was abstracted, and presently he said:

"Do you know, I fancy I was wrong in thinking that the waiter swore at me, and I'll withdraw my charge tomorrow."

Myddleton Finch then left me, and, sitting alone, I realised that I had been doing William a service. To some slight extent I may have intentionally helped him to retain his place in the club, and I now see the reason, which was that he alone knows precisely to what extent I like my claret heated.

For a mere second I remembered William's remark that

he should not be able to see the girl Jenny from the library windows. Then this recollection drove from my head that I had only dined in the sense that my dinner-bill was paid. Returning to the dining room, I happened to take my chair at the window, and while I was eating a deviled kidney I saw in the street the girl whose nods had such an absurd effect on William.

The children of the poor are as thoughtless as their parents, and this Jenny did not sign to the windows in the hope that William might see her, though she could not see him. Her face, which was disgracefully dirty, bore doubt and dismay on it, but whether she brought good news it would not tell. Somehow I had expected her to signal when she saw me, and, though her message could not interest me, I was in the mood in which one is irritated at that not taking place which he is awaiting. Ultimately she seemed to be making up her mind to go away.

A boy was passing with the evening papers, and I hurried out to get one, rather thoughtlessly, for we have all the papers in the club. Unfortunately, I misunderstood the direction the boy had taken; but round the first corner (out of sight of the club windows) I saw the girl Jenny, and so asked her how William's wife was.

"Did he send you to me?" she replied, impertinently taking me for a waiter. "My!" she added, after a second scrutiny, "I b'lieve you're one of them. His missis is a bit better, and I was to tell him as she took all the tapiocar."

"How could you tell him?" I asked.

"I was to do like this," she replied, and re-enacted the supping of something out of a plate.

"That would not show she ate all the tapioca," I said.

"But I was to end like this," she answered, licking an imaginary plate with her tongue.

I gave her a shilling (to get rid of her), and returned to the club disgusted.

Later in the evening I had to go to the club library for a book, and while William was looking in vain for it (I had forgotten the title) I said to him:

"By the way, William, Mr. Myddleton Finch is to tell the committee that he was mistaken in the charge he brought against you, so you will doubtless be restored to the dining room tomorrow."

The two members were still in their chairs, probably sleeping lightly; yet he had the effrontery to thank me.

"Don't thank me," I said, blushing at the imputation. "Remember your place, William!"

"But Mr. Myddleton Finch knew I swore," he insisted.

"A gentleman," I replied, stiffly, "cannot remember for twenty-four hours what a waiter has said to him."

"No, sir; but—"

To stop him I had to say: "And, ah, William, your wife is a little better. She has eaten the tapioca—all of it."

"How can you know, sir?"

"By an accident."

"Jenny signed to the window?"

"No."

"Then you saw her, and went out, and—"

"Nonsense!"

"Oh, sir, to do that for me! May God bl—"

"William!"

"Forgive me, sir; but—when I tell my missis, she will say it was thought of your own wife as made you do it."

He wrung my hand. I dared not withdraw it, lest we should waken the sleepers.

William returned to the dining room, and I had to show him that if he did not cease looking gratefully at me I must change my waiter. I also ordered him to stop telling me nightly how his wife was, but I continued to know, as I could not help seeing the girl Jenny from the window. Twice in a week I learned from this objectionable child that the ailing woman had again eaten all the tapioca. Then I became suspicious of William. I will tell why.

It began with a remark of Captain Upjohn's. We had been speaking of the inconvenience of not being able to get a hot dish served after 1 a.m. and he said:

"It is because these lazy waiters would strike. If the beggars had a love of their work they would not rush away from the club the moment one o'clock strikes. That glum fellow who often waits on you takes to his heels the moment he is clear of the club steps. He ran into me the other night at the top of the street, and was off without apologising."

"You mean the foot of the street, Upjohn," I said; for such is the way to Drury Lane.

"No; I mean the top. The man was running west."

"East."

"West."

I smiled, which so annoyed him that he bet me two to one in sovereigns. The bet could have been decided most quickly by asking William a question, but I thought, foolishly doubtless, that it might hurt his feelings, so I watched him leave the club. The possibility of Upjohn's winning the bet had seemed remote to me. Conceive my surprise, therefore when William went westward.

Amazed, I pursued him along two streets without realising that I was doing so. Then curiosity put me into a hansom. We followed William, and it proved to be a three-shilling fare, for, running when he was in breath and walking when he was out of it, he took me to West Kensington.

I discharged my cab, and from across the street watched William's incomprehensible behaviour. He had stopped at a dingy row of workmen's houses, and knocked at the darkened window of one of them. Presently a light showed. So far as I could see, someone pulled up the blind and for ten minutes talked to William. I was uncertain whether they talked, for the window was not opened, and I felt that, had William spoken through the glass loud enough to be heard inside, I must have heard him too. Yet he nodded and beckoned. I was still bewildered when, by setting off the way he had come, he gave me the opportunity of going home.

Knowing from the talk of the club what the lower orders are, could I doubt that this was some discreditable love affair of William's? His concern for his wife had been mere pretence; so far as it was genuine, it meant that he feared she might recover. He probably told her that he was detained nightly in the club till three.

I was miserable next day, and blamed the deviled kidneys for it. Whether William was unfaithful to his wife was nothing to me, but I had two plain reasons for insisting on his going straight home from his club: the one that, as he had made me lose a bet, I must punish him; the other that he could wait upon me better if he went to bed earlier.

Yet I did not question him. There was something in his face that—Well, I seemed to see his dying wife in it.

I was so out of sorts that I could eat no dinner. I left the club. Happening to stand for some time at the foot of the street, I chanced to see the girl Jenny coming, and—No; let me tell the truth, though the whole club reads: I was waiting for her.

"How is William's wife today?" I asked.

"She told me to nod three times," the little girl replied; "but she looked like nothink but a dead one till she got the brandy.

"Hush, child!" I said, shocked. "You don't know how the dead look."

"Bless yer," she answered, "don't I just! Why, I've helped to lay 'em out. I'm going on seven."

"Is William good to his wife?"

"Course he is. Ain't she his missis?"

"Why should that make him good to her?" I asked, cynically, out of my knowledge of the poor. But the girl, precocious in many ways, had never had any opportunities of studying the lower classes in the newspapers, fiction, and club talk. She shut one eye, and, looking up wonderingly, said:

"Ain't you green—just!"

"When does William reach home at night?"

"'Tain't night; it's morning. When I wakes up at half

dark and half light, and hears a door shutting, I know as it's either father going off to his work or Mr. Hicking come home from his."

"Who is Mr. Hicking?"

"Him as we've been speaking on—William. We calls him mister, 'cause he's a toff. Father's just doing jobs in Covent Gardens, but Mr. Hicking, he's a waiter, and a clean shirt every day. The old woman would like father to be a waiter, but he hain't got the 'ristocratic look."

"What old woman?"

"Go 'long! That's my mother. Is it true there's a waiter in the club just for to open the door?"

"Yes; but—"

"And another just for to lick the stamps? My!"

"William leaves the club at one o'clock?" I said, interrogatively.

She nodded. "My mother," she said, "is one to talk, and she says Mr. Hicking as he should get away at twelve, 'cause his missis needs him more'n the gentlemen need him. The old woman do talk."

"And what does William answer to that?"

"He says as the gentlemen can't be kept waiting for their cheese."

"But William does not go straight home when he leaves the club?"

"That's the kid."

"Kid!" I echoed, scarcely understanding, for, knowing how little the poor love their children, I had asked William no questions about the baby.

"Didn't you know his missis had a kid?"

"Yes; but that is no excuse for William's staying away from his sick wife," I answered, sharply. A baby in such a home as William's, I reflected, must be trying; but still — Besides, his class can sleep through any din.

"The kid ain't in our court," the girl explained. "He's in W., he is, and I've never been out of W.C.; leastwise, not as I knows on."

"This is W. I suppose you mean that the child is at West Kensington? Well, no doubt it was better for William's wife to get rid of the child—"

"Better!" interposed the girl. "'Tain't better for her not to have the kid. Ain't her not having him what she's always thinking on when she looks like a dead one?"

"How could you know that?"

"Cause," answered the girl, illustrating her words with a gesture, "I watches her, and I sees her arms going this way, just like as she wanted to hug her kid."

"Possibly you are right," I said, frowning; "but William had put the child out to nurse because it disturbed his night's rest. A man who has his work to do—"

"You are green!"

"Then why have the mother and child been separated?"

"Along of that there measles. Near all the young 'uns in our court has 'em bad."

"Have you had them?"

"I said the young 'uns."

"And William sent the baby to West Kensington to escape infection?"

"Took him, he did."

"Against his wife's wishes?"

"Na-o!"

"You said she was dying for want of the child?"

"Wouldn't she rather die than have the kid die?"

"Don't speak so heartlessly, child. Why does William not go straight home from the club? Does he go to West Kensington to see it?"

"Course he do."

"Then he should not. His wife has the first claim on him."

"Ain't you green! It's his missis as wants him to go. Do you think she could sleep till she knowed how the kid was?"

"But he does not go into the house at West Kensington?"

"Is he soft? Course he don't go in, fear of taking the infection to the kid. They just holds the kid up at the window to him, so as he can have a good look. Then he comes home and tells his missis. He sits foot of the bed and tells."

"And that takes place every night? He can't have much to tell."

"He has just."

"He can only say whether the child is well or ill."

"My! He tells what a difference there is in the kid since he seed him last."

"There can be no difference!"

"Go 'long! Ain't a kid always growing? Haven't Mr. Hicking to tell how the hair is getting darker, and heaps of things beside?"

"Such as what?"

"Like whether he larfed, and if he has her nose, and how as he knowed him. He tells her them things more 'n once."

"And all this time he is sitting at the foot of the bed?"

"'Cept when he holds her hand."

"But when does he get to bed himself?"

"He don't get much. He tells her as he has a sleep at the club."

"He cannot say that."

"Hain't I heard him? But he do go to his bed a bit, and then they both lies quiet, her pretending she is sleeping so as he can sleep, and him 'fraid to sleep case he shouldn't wake up to give her the bottle stuff."

"What does the doctor say about her?"

"He's a good one, the doctor. Sometimes he says she would get better if she could see the kid through the window."

"Nonsense!"

"And if she was took to the country."

"Then why does not William take her?"

"My! You are green! And if she drank port wines."

"Doesn't she?"

"No; but William, he tells her about the gentlemen drinking them."

On the tenth day after my conversation with this unattractive child I was in my brougham, with the windows up, and I sat back, a paper before my face lest any one should look in. Naturally, I was afraid of being seen in company of William's wife and Jenny, for men about town are uncharitable, and, despite the explanation I had ready, might have charged me with pitying William. As a matter of fact, William was sending his wife into Surrey to stay with an old nurse of mine, and I was driving her down because my horses needed an outing. Besides, I was going that way at any rate.

I had arranged that the girl Jenny, who was wearing an outrageous bonnet, should accompany us, because, knowing the greed of her class, I feared she might blackmail me at the club.

William joined us in the suburbs, bringing the baby with him, as I had foreseen they would all be occupied with it, and to save me the trouble of conversing with them. Mrs. Hicking I found too pale and fragile for a workingman's wife, and I formed a mean opinion of her intelligence from her pride in the baby, which was a very ordinary one. She created quite a vulgar scene when it was brought to her, though she had given me her word not to do so, what irritated me even more than her tears being her ill-bred apology that she "had 'feared baby wouldn't know her again." I would have told her they didn't know anyone for years had I not been afraid of the girl Jenny, who dandled the infant on her knees and talked to it as if it understood. She kept me on tenterhooks by asking it offensive questions, such as, "'Oo know who give me that bonnet?" and answering them herself, "It was the pretty gentleman there;" and several times I had to affect sleep because she announced, "Kiddy wants to kiss the pretty gentleman."

Irksome as all this necessarily was to a man of taste, I suffered even more when we reached our destination. As we drove through the village the girl Jenny uttered shrieks of delight at the sight of flowers growing up the cottage walls, and declared they were "just like a music' all without the drink license." As my horses required a rest, I was forced to abandon my intention of dropping these persons at their lodgings and returning to town at once, and I could not go to the inn lest I should meet inquisitive acquaintances. Disagreeable circumstances, therefore, compelled me to take tea with a waiter's family—close to a window too, through which I could see the girl Jenny talking excitedly to the villagers, and telling them, I felt certain, that I had been good to William. I had a desire to go out and put myself right with those people.

William's long connection with the club should have given him some manners, but apparently his class cannot take them on, for, though he knew I regarded his thanks as an insult, he looked them when he was not speaking them, and hardly had he sat down, by my orders, than he remembered that I was a member of the club, and jumped up. Nothing is in worse form than whispering, yet again and again, when he thought I was not listening, he whispered to Mrs. Hicking, "You don't feel faint?" or "How are you now?" He was also in extravagant glee because she ate two cakes (it takes so little to put these people in good spirits), and when she said she felt like another being already the fellow's face charged me with the change. I could not but conclude, from the way Mrs. Hicking let the baby pound her, that she was stronger than she had pretended.

I remained longer than was necessary, because I had

something to say to William which I knew he would misunderstand, and so I put off saying it. But when he announced that it was time for him to return to London,—at which his wife suddenly paled, so that he had to sign to her not to break down,—I delivered the message.

"William," I said, "the head waiter asked me to say that you could take a fortnight's holiday just now. Your wages will be paid as usual."

Confound them! William had me by the hand, and his wife was in tears before I could reach the door.

"Is it your doing again, sir?" William cried.

"William!" I said, fiercely.

"We owe everything to you," he insisted. "The port wine—"

"Because I had no room for it in my cellar."

"The money for the nurse in London—"

"Because I objected to being waited on by a man who got no sleep."

"These lodgings—"

"Because I wanted to do something for my old nurse."

"And now, sir, a fortnight's holiday!"

"Goodbye, William!" I said, in a fury.

But before I could get away Mrs. Hicking signed to William to leave the room, and then she kissed my hand. She said something to me. It was about my wife. Somehow I—What business had William to tell her about my wife?

They are all back in Drury Lane now, and William tells me that his wife sings at her work just as she did eight years ago. I have no interest in this, and try to check his talk of it; but such people have no sense of propriety, and he even speaks of the girl Jenny, who sent me lately a gaudy pair of worsted gloves worked by her own hand. The meanest advantage they took of my weakness, however, was in calling their baby after me. I have an uncomfortable suspicion, too, that William has given the other waiters his version of the affair; but I feel safe so long as it does not reach the committee.

LAURA

by Saki

"You are not really dying, are you?" asked Amanda.

"I have the doctor's permission to live till Tuesday," said Laura.

"But today is Saturday; this is serious!" gasped Amanda.

"I don't know about it being serious; it is certainly Saturday," said Laura.

"Death is always serious," said Amanda.

"I never said I was going to die. I am presumably going to leave off being Laura, but I shall go on being something. An animal of some kind, I suppose. You see, when one hasn't been very good in the life one has just lived, one reincarnates in some lower organism. And I haven't been very good, when one comes to think of it. I've been petty and mean and vindictive and all that sort of thing when circumstances have seemed to warrant it."

"Circumstances never warrant that sort of thing," said Amanda hastily.

"If you don't mind my saying so," observed Laura, "Egbert is a circumstance that would warrant any amount of that sort of thing. You're married to him—that's different; you've sworn to love, honour, and endure him: I haven't."

"I don't see what's wrong with Egbert," protested Amanda.

"Oh, I daresay the wrongness has been on my part," admitted Laura dispassionately; "he has merely been the extenuating circumstance. He made a thin, peevish kind of fuss, for instance, when I took the collie puppies from the farm out for a run the other day."

"They chased his young broods of speckled Sussex and drove two sitting hens off their nests, besides running all over the flower beds. You know how devoted he is to his poultry and garden."

"Anyhow, he needn't have gone on about it for the entire evening and then have said, 'Let's say no more about it' just when I was beginning to enjoy the discussion. That's where one of my petty vindictive revenges came in," added Laura with an unrepentant chuckle; "I turned the entire family of speckled Sussex into his seedling shed the day after the puppy episode."

"How could you?" exclaimed Amanda.

"It came quite easy," said Laura; "two of the hens pretended to be laying at the time, but I was firm."

"And we thought it was an accident!"

"You see," resumed Laura, "I really *have* some grounds for supposing that my next incarnation will be in a lower organism. I shall be an animal of some kind. On the other hand, I haven't been a bad sort in my way, so I think I may count on being a nice animal, something elegant and lively, with a love of fun. An otter, perhaps."

"I can't imagine you as an otter," said Amanda.

"Well, I don't suppose you can imagine me as an angel, if it comes to that," said Laura.

Amanda was silent. She couldn't.

"Personally I think an otter life would be rather enjoyable," continued Laura; "salmon to eat all the year round, and the satisfaction of being able to fetch the trout in their own homes without having to wait for hours till they condescend to rise to the fly you've been dangling before them; and an elegant svelte figure—"

"Think of the otter hounds," interposed Amanda; "how dreadful to be hunted and harried and finally worried to death!"

"Rather fun with half the neighbourhood looking on, and anyhow not worse than this Saturday-to-Tuesday business of dying by inches; and then I should go on into something else. If I had been a moderately good otter I suppose I should get back into human shape; probably a little African boy, I should think."

"I wish you would be serious," sighed Amanda; "you really ought to be if you're only going to live till Tuesday."

As a matter of fact Laura died on Monday.

"So dreadfully upsetting," Amanda complained to her uncle-in-law, Sir Lulworth Quayne. "I've asked quite a lot of people down for golf and fishing, and the rhododendrons are just looking their best."

"Laura always was inconsiderate," said Sir Lulworth; "she was born during Goodwood week, with an Ambassador staying in the house who hated babies."

"She had the maddest kind of ideas," said Amanda. "She had an idea that she was going to be reincarnated as an otter."

"One meets with those ideas of reincarnation so frequently, even in the West," said Sir Lulworth. "And Laura was such an unaccountable person in this life that I should not like to lay down definite rules as to what she might be doing in an after state."

"You think she really might have passed into some animal form?" asked Amanda. She was one of those who shape their opinions rather readily from the standpoint of those around them.

Just then Egbert entered the breakfast room, wearing an air of bereavement that Laura's demise would have been insufficient, in itself, to account for.

"Four of my speckled Sussex have been killed," he exclaimed; "the very four that were to go to the show on Friday. One of them was dragged away and eaten right in the middle of that new carnation bed that I've been to such trouble and expense over. My best flower bed and my best fowls singled out for destruction; it almost seems as if the brute that did the deed had special knowledge how to be as devastating as possible in a short space of time."

"Was it a fox, do you think?" asked Amanda.

"Sounds more like a polecat," said Sir Lulworth.

"No," said Egbert, "there were marks of webbed feet all over the place, and we followed the tracks down to the stream at the bottom of the garden; evidently an otter."

Amanda looked quickly and furtively across at Sir Lulworth.

Egbert was too agitated to eat any breakfast, and went out to superintend the strengthening of the poultry yard defences.

"I think she might at least have waited till the funeral was over," said Amanda in a scandalised voice.

"It's her own funeral, you know," said Sir Lulworth; "it's a nice point in etiquette how far one ought to show respect to one's own mortal remains."

Disregard for mortuary convention was carried to further lengths next day; during the absence of the family at the funeral ceremony the remaining survivors of the speckled Sussex were massacred. The marauder's line of retreat seemed to have embraced most of the flowerbeds on the lawn, but the strawberry beds in the lower garden had also suffered.

"I shall get the otter hounds to come here at the earliest possible moment," said Egbert savagely.

"On no account! You can't dream of such a thing!" exclaimed Amanda. "I mean, it wouldn't do, so soon after a funeral in the house."

"It's a case of necessity," said Egbert; "once an otter takes to that sort of thing it won't stop."

"Perhaps it will go elsewhere now there are no more fowls left," suggested Amanda.

"One would think you wanted to shield the beast," said

Egbert.

"There's been so little water in the stream lately," objected Amanda; "it seems hardly sporting to hunt an animal when it has so little chance of taking refuge anywhere."

"Good gracious!" fumed Egbert, "I'm not thinking about sport. I want to have the animal killed as soon as possible."

Even Amanda's opposition weakened when, during church time on the following Sunday, the otter made its way into the house, raided half a salmon from the larder and tore it into scaly fragments on the Persian rug in Egbert's studio.

"We shall have it hiding under our beds and biting pieces out of our feet before long," said Egbert, and from what Amanda knew of this particular otter she felt that the possibility was not a remote one.

On the evening preceding the day fixed for the hunt Amanda spent a solitary hour walking by the banks of the stream, making what she imagined to be hound noises. It was charitably supposed by those who overheard her performance, that she was practising for farmyard imitations at the forthcoming village entertainment.

It was her friend and neighbour, Aurora Burret, who brought her news of the day's sport.

"Pity you weren't out; we had quite a good day. We found it at once, in the pool just below your garden."

"Did you—kill?" asked Amanda.

"Rather. A fine she-otter. Your husband got rather badly bitten in trying to 'tail it.' Poor beast, I felt quite sorry for it, it had such a human look in its eyes when it was killed. You'll call me silly, but do you know who the look reminded me of? My dear woman, what is the matter?"

When Amanda had recovered to a certain extent from her attack of nervous prostration Egbert took her to the Nile Valley to recuperate. Change of scene speedily brought about the desired recovery of health and mental balance. The escapades of an adventurous otter in search of a variation of diet were viewed in their proper light. Amanda's normally placid temperament reasserted itself. Even a hurricane of shouted curses, coming from her husband's dressing room, in her husband's voice, but hardly in his usual vocabulary, failed to disturb her serenity as she made a leisurely toilet one evening in a Cairo hotel.

"What is the matter? What has happened?" she asked in amused curiosity.

"The little beast has thrown all my clean shirts into the bath! Wait till I catch you, you little—"

"What little beast?" asked Amanda, suppressing a desire to laugh; Egbert's language was so hopelessly inadequate to express his outraged feelings.

"A little beast of an African boy," spluttered Egbert.

And now Amanda is seriously ill.

THE GREY PARROT

by W. W. Jacobs

The Chief engineer and the Third sat at tea on the S. S. Curlew in the East India Docks. The two men ate steadily, conversing between bites, and interrupted occasionally by a hoarse and solemn voice, the owner of which, being much exercised by the sight of the food, asked for it, prettily at first, and afterwards in a way which at least compelled attention.

"That's pretty good for a parrot," said the Third critically. "Seems to know what he's saying too. No, don't give it anything. It'll stop if you do."

"There's no pleasure to me in listening to coarse language," said the Chief with dignity.

He absently dipped a piece of bread and butter in the Third's tea, and losing it chased it round and round the bottom of the cap with his finger, the Third regarding the operation with an interest and emotion which he was at first unable to understand.

"You'd better pour yourself out another cup," he said thoughtfully as he caught the Third's eye.

"I'm going to," said the other dryly.

"The man I bought it off," said the Chief, giving the bird the sop, "said that it was a perfectly respectable parrot and wouldn't know a bad word if it heard it. I hardly like to give it to my wife now."

"It's no good being too particular," said the Third, regarding him with an ill-concealed grin; "that's the worst of all you young married fellows. Seem to think your wife has got to be wrapped up in brown paper. Ten chances to one she'll be amused."

The Chief shrugged his shoulders disdainfully. "I bought the bird to be company for her," he said slowly; "she'll be very lonesome without me, Rogers."

"How do you know?" inquired the other.

"She said so," was the reply.

"When you've been married as long as I have," said the Third, who having been married some fifteen years felt that their usual positions were somewhat reversed, "you'll know that generally speaking they're glad to get rid of you."

"What for?" demanded the Chief in a voice that Othello might have envied.

"Well, you get in the way a bit," said Rogers with secret enjoyment; "you see you upset the arrangements. House cleaning and all that sort of thing gets interrupted. They're glad to see you back at first, and then glad to see the back of you."

"There's wives and wives," said the bridegroom tenderly.

"And mine's a good one," said the Third, "registered A1 at Lloyd's, but she don't worry about me going away. Your wife's thirty years younger than you, isn't she?"

"Twenty-five," corrected the other shortly. "You see what I'm afraid of is, that she'll get too much attention."

"Well, women like that," remarked the Third.

"But I don't, damn it," cried the Chief hotly. "When I think of it I get hot all over. Boiling hot."

"That won't last," said the other reassuringly; "you won't care twopence this time next year."

"We're not all alike," growled the Chief; "some of us have got finer feelings than others have. I saw the chap next door looking at her as we passed him this morning."

"Lor'," said the Third.

"I don't want any of your damned impudence," said the Chief sharply. "He put his hat on straighter when he passed us. What do you think of that?"

"Can't say," replied the other with commendable gravity; "it might mean anything."

"If he has any of his nonsense while I'm away I'll break his neck," said the Chief passionately. "I shall know of it."

The other raised his eyebrows.

"I've asked the landlady to keep her eyes open a bit," said the Chief. "My wife was brought up in the country, and she's very young and simple, so that it is quite right and proper for her to have a motherly old body to look after her."

"Told your wife?" queried Rogers.

"No," said the other. "Fact is, I've got an idea about that parrot. I'm going to tell her it's a magic bird, and will tell me everything she does while I'm away. Anything the landlady tells me I shall tell her I got from the parrot. For one thing, I don't want her to go out after seven of an evening, and she's promised me she won't. If she does I shall know, and pretend that I know through the parrot. What do you think of it?"

"Think of it?" said the Third, staring at him. "Think of it? Fancy a man telling a grown-up woman a yarn like that!"

"She believes in warnings and death-watches, and all that sort of thing," said the Chief, "so why shouldn't she?"

"Well, you'll know whether she believes in it or not when you come back," said Rogers, "and it'll be a great pity, because it's a beautiful talker."

"What do you mean?" said the other.

"I mean it'll get its little neck wrung," said the Third.

"Well, we'll see," said Gannett. "I shall know what to think if it does die."

"I shall never see that bird again," said Rogers, shaking his head as the Chief took up the cage and handed it to the steward, who was to accompany him home with it.

The couple left the ship and proceeded down the East India Dock Road side by side, the only incident being a hot argument between a constable and the engineer as to whether he could or could not be held responsible for the language in which the parrot saw fit to indulge when the steward happened to drop it.

The engineer took the cage at his door, and, not without some misgivings, took it upstairs into the parlour and set it on the table. Mrs. Gannett, a simple-looking woman, with sleepy brown eyes and a docile manner, clapped her hands with joy.

"Isn't it a beauty?" said Mr. Gannett, looking at it; "I bought it to be company for you while I'm away."

"You're too good to me, Jem," said his wife. She walked all round the cage admiring it, the parrot, which was of a highly suspicious and nervous disposition, having had boys at its last place, turning with her. After she had walked round him five times he got sick of it, and in a simple sailorly fashion said so.

"Oh, Jem," said his wife.

"It's a beautiful talker," said Gannett hastily, "and it's so clever that it picks up everything it hears, but it'll soon forget it."

"It looks as though it knows what you are saying," said his wife. "Just look at it, the artful thing."

The opportunity was too good to be missed, and in a few straightforward lies the engineer acquainted Mrs. Gannett of the miraculous powers with which he had chosen to endow it.

"But you don't believe it?" said his wife, staring at him open-mouthed.

"I do," said the engineer firmly.

"But how can it know what I'm doing when I'm away?" persisted Mrs. Gannett.

"Ah, that's its secret," said the engineer; "a good many people would like to know that, but nobody has found out yet. It's a magic bird, and when you've said that you've said all there is to say about it."

Mrs. Gannett, wrinkling her forehead, eyed the marvellous bird curiously.

"You'll find it's quite true," said Gannett; "when I come back that bird'll be able to tell me how you've been and all about you. Everything you've done during my absence."

"Good gracious!" said the astonished Mrs. Gannett.

"If you stay out after seven of an evening, or do anything else that I shouldn't like, that bird'll tell me," continued the engineer impressively. "It'll tell me who comes to see you, and in fact it will tell me everything you do while I'm away."

"Well, it won't have anything bad to tell of me," said Mrs. Gannett composedly, "unless it tells lies."

"It can't tell lies," said her husband confidently, "and now, if you go and put your bonnet on, we'll drop in at the theatre for half an hour."

It was a prophetic utterance, for he made such a fuss over the man next to his wife offering her his opera-glasses, that they left, at the urgent request of the management, in almost exactly that space of time.

"You'd better carry me about in a bandbox," said Mrs. Gannett wearily as the outraged engineer stalked home beside her. "What harm was the man doing?"

"You must have given him some encouragement," said Mr. Gannett fiercely—"made eyes at him or something. A man wouldn't offer to lend a lady his opera-glasses without."

Mrs. Gannett tossed her head—and that so decidedly,

that a passing stranger turned his head and looked at her. Mr. Gannett accelerated his pace, and taking his wife's arm, led her swiftly home with a passion too great for words.

By the morning his anger had evaporated, but his misgivings remained. He left after breakfast for the Curlew, which was to sail in the afternoon, leaving behind him copious instructions, by following which his wife would be enabled to come down and see him off with the minimum exposure of her fatal charms.

Left to herself Mrs. Gannett dusted the room, until, coming to the parrot's cage, she put down the duster and eyed its eerie occupant curiously. She fancied that she saw an evil glitter in the creature's eye, and the knowing way in which it drew the film over it was as near an approach to a wink as a bird could get.

She was still looking at it when there was a knock at the door, and a bright little woman—rather smartly dressed—bustled into the room, and greeted her effusively.

"I just came to see you, my dear, because I thought a little outing would do me good," she said briskly; "and if you've no objection I'll come down to the docks with you to see the boat off."

Mrs. Gannett assented readily. It would ease the engineer's mind, she thought, if he saw her with a chaperon.

"Nice bird," said Mrs. Cluffins, mechanically bringing her parasol to the charge.

"Don't do that," said her friend hastily.

"Why not?" said the other.

"Language!" said Mrs. Gannett solemnly.

"Well, I must do something to it," said Mrs. Cluffins restlessly.

She held the parasol near the cage and suddenly opened it. It was a flaming scarlet, and for the moment the shock took the parrot's breath away.

"He don't mind that," said Mrs. Gannett.

The parrot, hopping to the farthest corner of the bottom of his cage, said something feebly. Finding that nothing dreadful happened, he repeated his remark somewhat more boldly, and, being convinced after all that the apparition was quite harmless and that he had displayed his craven spirit for nothing, hopped back on his perch and raved wickedly.

"If that was my bird," said Mrs. Cluffins, almost as scarlet as her parasol, "I should wring its neck."

"No, you wouldn't," said Mrs. Gannett solemnly. And having quieted the bird by throwing a cloth over its cage, she explained its properties.

"What!" said Mrs. Cluffins, unable to sit still in her chair. "You mean to tell me your husband said that!"

Mrs. Gannett nodded.

"He's awfully jealous of me," she said with a slight simper.

"I wish he was my husband," said Mrs. Cluffins in a thin, hard voice. "I wish C. would talk to me like that."

"It shows he's fond of me," said Mrs. Gannett, looking down.

Mrs. Cluffins jumped up, and snatching the cover off the cage, endeavoured, but in vain, to get the parasol through the bars.

"And you believe that rubbish!" she said scathingly. "Boo, you wretch!"

"I don't believe it," said her friend, taking her gently away and covering the cage hastily just as the bird was recovering, "but I let him think I do."

"I call it an outrage," said Mrs. Cluffins, waving the parasol wildly. "I never heard of such a thing; I'd like to give Mr. Gannett a piece of my mind. Just about half an hour of it. He wouldn't be the same man afterwards—I'd parrot him."

Mrs. Gannett, soothing her agitated friend as well as she was able, led her gently to a chair and removed her bonnet, and finding that complete recovery was impossible while the parrot remained in the room, took that wonder-working bird outside.

By the time they had reached the docks and boarded the Curlew Mrs. Cluffins had quite recovered her spirits. She roamed about the steamer asking questions, which savoured more of idle curiosity than a genuine thirst for knowledge, and was at no pains to conceal her opinion of those who were unable to furnish her with satisfactory replies.

"I shall think of you every day, Jem," said Mrs. Gannett tenderly.

"I shall think of you every minute," said the engineer reproachfully.

He sighed gently and gazed in a scandalised fashion at Mrs. Cluffins, who was carrying on a desperate flirtation with one of the apprentices.

"She's very light-hearted," said his wife, following the direction of his eyes.

"She is," said Mr. Gannett curtly, as the unconscious Mrs. Cluffins shut her parasol and rapped the apprentice playfully with the handle. "She seems to be on very good terms with Jenkins, laughing and carrying on. I don't suppose she's ever seen him before."

"Poor young things," said Mrs. Cluffins solemnly, as she came up to them. "Don't you worry, Mr. Gannett; I'll look after her and keep her from moping."

"You're very kind," said the engineer slowly.

"We'll have a jolly time," said Mrs. Cluffins. "I often wish my husband was a seafaring man. A wife does have more freedom, doesn't she?"

"More what?" inquired Mr. Gannett huskily.

"More freedom," said Mrs. Cluffins gravely. "I always envy sailors' wives. They can do as they like. No husband to look after them for nine or ten months in the year."

Before the unhappy engineer could put his indignant thoughts into words there was a warning cry from the gangway, and with a hasty farewell he hurried below. The visitors went ashore, the gangway was shipped, and in response to the clang of the telegraph the Curlew drifted slowly away from the quay and headed for the swing-bridge slowly opening in front of her.

The two ladies hurried to the pier-head and watched the steamer down the river until a bend hid it from view. Then Mrs. Gannett, with a sensation of having lost something, due, so her friend assured her, to the want of a cup of tea, went slowly back to her lonely home.

In the period of grass-widowhood which ensued, Mrs. Cluffins's visits formed almost the sole relief to the bare monotony of existence. As a companion the parrot was an utter failure, its language being so irredeemably bad that it spent most of its time in the spare room with a cloth over its cage, wondering when the days were going to lengthen a bit. Mrs. Cluffins suggested selling it, but her friend repelled the suggestion with horror, and refused to entertain it at any price, even that of the publican at the corner, who, having heard of the bird's command of language, was bent upon buying it.

"I wonder what that beauty will have to tell your husband," said Mrs. Cluffins, as they sat together one day some three months after the Curlew's departure.

"I should hope that he has forgotten that nonsense," said Mrs. Gannett, reddening; "he never alludes to it in his letters."

"Sell it," said Mrs. Cluffins peremptorily. "It's no good to you, and Hobson would give anything for it almost."

Mrs. Gannett shook her head. "The house wouldn't hold my husband if I did," she remarked with a shiver.

"Oh, yes, it would," said Mrs. Cluffins; "you do as I tell you, and a much smaller house than this would hold him. I told C. to tell Hobson he should have it for five pounds."

"But he mustn't," said her friend in alarm.

"Leave yourself right in my hands," said Mrs. Cluffins, spreading out two small palms and regarding them complacently. "It'll be all right, I promise you."

She put her arm round her friend's waist and led her to the window, talking earnestly. In five minutes Mrs.

Gannett was wavering, in ten she had given way, and in fifteen the energetic Mrs. Cluffins was en route for Hobson's, swinging the cage so violently in her excitement that the parrot was reduced to holding on to its perch with claws and bill. Mrs. Gannett watched the progress from the window, and with a strange look on her face sat down to think out the points of attack and defence in the approaching fray.

A week later a four-wheeler drove up to the door, and the engineer, darting upstairs three steps at a time, dropped an armful of parcels on the floor, and caught his wife in an embrace which would have done credit to a bear. Mrs. Gannett, for reasons of which lack of muscle was only one, responded less ardently.

"Ha, it's good to be home again," said Gannett, sinking into an easy-chair and pulling his wife on his knee. "And how have you been? Lonely?"

"I got used to it," said Mrs. Gannett softly.

The engineer coughed. "You had the parrot," he remarked.

"Yes, I had the magic parrot," said Mrs. Gannett.

"How's it getting on?" said her husband, looking round. "Where is it?"

"Part of it is on the mantelpiece," said Mrs. Gannett, trying to speak calmly, "part of it is in a bonnet-box upstairs, some of it's in my pocket, and here is the remainder."

She fumbled in her pocket and placed in his hand a cheap two-bladed clasp knife.

"On the mantelpiece!" repeated the engineer staring at

the knife; "in a bonnet-box!"

"Those blue vases," said his wife. Mr. Gannett put his hand to his head. If he had heard right one parrot had changed into a pair of vases, a bonnet, and a knife. A magic bird with a vengeance.

"I sold it," said Mrs. Gannett suddenly.

The engineer's knee stiffened inhospitably, and his arm dropped from his wife's waist. She rose quietly and took a chair opposite.

"Sold it!" said Mr. Gannett in awful tones. "Sold my parrot!"

"I didn't like it, Jem," said his wife. "I didn't want that bird watching me, and I did want the vases, and the bonnet, and the little present for you."

Mr. Gannett pitched the little present to the other end of the room.

"You see it mightn't have told the truth, Jem," continued Mrs. Gannett. "It might have told all sorts of lies about me, and made no end of mischief."

"It couldn't lie," shouted the engineer passionately, rising from his chair and pacing the room. "It's your guilty conscience that's made a coward of you. How dare you sell my parrot?"

"Because it wasn't truthful, Jem," said his wife, who was somewhat pale.

"If you were half as truthful you'd do," vociferated the engineer, standing over her. "You, you deceitful woman."

Mrs. Gannett fumbled in her pocket again, and producing a small handkerchief applied it delicately to her eyes.

"I—I got rid of it for your sake," she stammered. "It used to tell such lies about you. I couldn't bear to listen to it."

"About me!" said Mr. Gannett, sinking into his seat and staring at his wife with very natural amazement. "Tell lies about me! Nonsense! How could it?"

"I suppose it could tell me about you as easily as it could tell you about me?" said Mrs. Gannett. "There was more magic in that bird than you thought, Jem. It used to say shocking things about you. I couldn't bear it."

"Do you think you're talking to a child or a fool?" demanded the engineer.

Mrs. Gannett shook her head feebly. She still kept the handkerchief to her eyes, but allowed a portion to drop over her mouth.

"I should like to hear some of the stories it told about me—if you can remember them," said the engineer with bitter sarcasm.

"The first lie," said Mrs. Gannett in a feeble but ready voice, "was about the time you were at Genoa. The parrot said you were at some concert gardens at the upper end of the town."

One moist eye coming mildly from behind the handkerchief saw the engineer stiffen suddenly in his chair.

"I don't suppose there even is such a place," she continued.

"I—b'leve—there—is," said her husband jerkily. "I've heard—our chaps—talk of it."

"But you haven't been there?" said his wife anxiously.

"Never!" said the engineer with extraordinary vehemence.

"That wicked bird said that you got intoxicated there," said Mrs. Gannett in solemn accents, "that you smashed a little marble-topped table and knocked down two waiters, and that if it hadn't been for the captain of the Pursuit, who was in there and who got you away, you'd have been locked up. Wasn't it a wicked bird?"

"Horrible!" said the engineer huskily.

"I don't suppose there ever was a ship called the Pursuit," continued Mrs. Gannett.

"Doesn't sound like a ship's name," murmured Mr. Gannett.

"Well, then, a few days later it said the Curlew was at Naples."

"I never went ashore all the time we were at Naples," remarked the engineer casually.

"The parrot said you did," said Mrs. Gannett.

"I suppose you'll believe your own lawful husband before that damned bird?" shouted Gannett, starting up.

"Of course I didn't believe it, Jem," said his wife. "I'm trying to prove to you that the bird was not truthful, but you're so hard to persuade."

Mr. Gannett took a pipe from his pocket, and with a small knife dug with much severity and determination a hardened plug from the bowl, and blew noisily through the stem.

"There was a girl kept a fruit stall just by the harbour," said Mrs. Gannett, "and on this evening, on the strength of having bought three-pennyworth of green figs, you put your arm round her waist and tried to kiss her, and her sweetheart, who was standing close by, tried to stab you. The parrot said that you were in such a state of terror that you jumped into the harbour and were nearly drowned."

Mr. Gannett having loaded his pipe lit it slowly and carefully, and with tidy precision got up and deposited the match in the fireplace.

"It used to frighten me so with its stories that I hardly knew what to do with myself," continued Mrs. Gannett "When you were at Suez—"

The engineer waved his hand imperiously.

"That's enough," he said stiffly.

"I'm sure I don't want to have to repeat what it told me about Suez," said his wife. "I thought you'd like to hear it, that's all."

"Not at all," said the engineer, puffing at his pipe. "Not at all."

"But you see why I got rid of the bird, don't you?" said Mrs. Gannett. "If it had told you untruths about me, you would have believed them, wouldn't you?"

Mr. Gannett took his pipe from his mouth and took his wife in his extended arms. "No, my dear," he said brokenly, "no more than you believe all this stuff about me."

"And I did quite right to sell it, didn't I, Jem?"

"Quite right," said Mr. Gannett with a great assumption of heartiness. "Best thing to do with it."

"You haven't heard the worst yet," said Mrs. Gannett. "When you were at Suez—"

Mr. Gannett consigned Suez to its only rival, and

thumping the table with his clenched fist, forbade his wife to mention the word again, and desired her to prepare supper.

Not until he heard his wife moving about in the kitchen below did he relax the severity of his countenance. Then his expression changed to one of extreme anxiety, and he restlessly paced the room seeking for light. It came suddenly.

"Jenkins," he gasped, "Jenkins and Mrs. Cluffins, and I was going to tell Cluffins about him writing to his wife. I expect he knows the letter by heart."

THE AWFUL FATE OF MELPOMENUS JONES

by Stephen Leacock

Some people—not you nor I, because we are so awfully self-possessed—but some people, find great difficulty in saying goodbye when making a call or spending the evening. As the moment draws near when the visitor feels that he is fairly entitled to go away he rises and says abruptly, "Well, I think I..." Then the people say, "Oh, must you go now? Surely it's early yet!" And a pitiful struggle ensues.

I think the saddest case of this kind of thing that I ever knew was that of my poor friend Melpomenus Jones, a curate—such a dear young man, and only twenty-three! He simply couldn't get away from people. He was too modest to tell a lie, and too religious to wish to appear rude. Now it happened that he went to call on some friends of his on the very first afternoon of his summer vacation. The next six weeks were entirely his own—absolutely nothing to do. He chatted awhile, drank two cups of tea, then braced himself for the effort and said suddenly:

"Well, I think I..."

But the lady of the house said, "Oh, no! Mr. Jones, can't you really stay a little longer?"

Jones was always truthful. "Oh, yes," he said, "of course, I—er—can stay."

"Then please don't go."

He stayed. He drank eleven cups of tea. Night was falling. He rose again.

"Well now," he said shyly, "I think I really..."

"You must go?" said the lady politely. "I thought perhaps you could have stayed to dinner..."

"Oh well, so I could, you know," Jones said, "if..."

"Then please stay, I'm sure my husband will be delighted."

"All right," he said feebly, "I'll stay," and he sank back into his chair, just full of tea, and miserable.

Papa came home. They had dinner. All through the meal Jones sat planning to leave at eight-thirty. All the family wondered whether Mr. Jones was stupid and sulky, or only stupid.

After dinner mamma undertook to "draw him out," and showed him photographs. She showed him all the family museum,—photos of papa's uncle and his wife, and mamma's brother and his little boy, an awfully interesting photo of papa's uncle's friend in his Bengal uniform, an awfully well-taken photo of papa's grandfather's partner's dog, and an awfully wicked one of papa as the devil for a fancy-dress ball. At eight-thirty Jones had examined seventy-one photographs. There were about sixty-nine more that he hadn't. Jones rose.

"I must say goodnight now," he pleaded.

"Say goodnight!" they said, "why it's only half-past eight! Have you anything to do?"

"Nothing," he admitted, and muttered something about staying six weeks, and then laughed miserably.

Just then it turned out that the favourite child of the family, such a dear little romp, had hidden Mr. Jones's hat; so papa said that he must stay, and invited him to a pipe and a chat. Papa had the pipe and gave Jones the chat, and still he stayed. Every moment he meant to take the plunge, but couldn't. Then papa began to get very tired of Jones, and fidgeted and finally said, with jocular irony, that Jones had better stay all night, they could give him a shake-down. Jones mistook his meaning and thanked him with tears in his eyes, and papa put Jones to bed in the spare room and cursed him heartily.

After breakfast next day, papa went off to his work in the city, and left Jones playing with the baby, broken-hearted. His nerve was utterly gone. He was meaning to leave all day, but the thing had got on his mind and he simply couldn't. When papa came home in the evening he was surprised and chagrined to find Jones still there. He thought to jockey him out with a jest, and said he thought he'd have to charge him for his board, he, he! The unhappy young man stared wildly for a moment, then wrung papa's hand, paid him a month's board in advance, and broke down and sobbed like a child.

In the days that followed he was moody and unapproachable. He lived, of course, entirely in the drawing room, and the lack of air and exercise began to tell sadly on his health. He passed his time in drinking tea and looking at the photographs. He would stand for hours gazing at the photographs of papa's uncle's friend in his Bengal uniform — talking to it, sometimes swearing bitterly at it. His mind was visibly failing.

At length the crash came. They carried him upstairs in a raging delirium of fever. The illness that followed was terrible. He recognized no one, not even papa's uncle's friend in his Bengal uniform. At times he would start up from his bed and shriek, "Well, I think I..." and then fall back upon the pillow with a horrible laugh. Then, again, he would leap up and cry, "Another cup of tea and more photographs! More photographs! Har! Har!"

At length, after a month of agony, on the last day of his vacation, he passed away. They say that when the last moment came, he sat up in bed with a beautiful smile of confidence playing upon his face, and said, "Well — the angels are calling me; I'm afraid I really must go now. Good afternoon."

And the rushing of his spirit from its prison-house was as rapid as a hunted cat passing over a garden fence.

WHAT STUMPED THE BLUE JAYS

by Mark Twain

Animals talk to each other, of course. There can be no question about that; but I suppose there are very few people who can understand them. I never knew but one man who could. I knew he could, however, because he told me so himself. He was a middle-aged, simple-hearted miner who had lived in a lonely corner of California, among the woods and mountains, a good many years, and had studied the ways of his only neighbors, the beasts and the birds, until he believed he could accurately translate any remark which they made. This was Jim Baker.

According to Jim Baker, some animals have only a limited education, and some use only simple words, and scarcely ever a comparison or a flowery figure; whereas, certain other animals have a large vocabulary, a fine command of language and a ready and fluent delivery;

consequently these latter talk a great deal; they like it; they are so conscious of their talent, and they enjoy "showing off." Baker said, that after long and careful observation, he had come to the conclusion that the blue jays were the best talkers he had found among birds and beasts. Said he:

"There's more to a blue jay than any other creature. He has got more moods, and more different kinds of feelings than other creatures; and, mind you, whatever a blue jay feels, he can put into language. And no mere commonplace language, either, but rattling, out-and-out book-talk—and bristling with metaphor, too—just bristling! And as for command of language—why *you* never see a blue jay get stuck for a word. No man ever did. They just boil out of him! And another thing: I've noticed a good deal, and there's no bird, or cow, or anything that uses as good grammar as a blue jay. You may say a cat uses good grammar. Well, a cat does—but you let a cat get excited once; you let a cat get to pulling fur with another cat on a shed, nights, and you'll hear grammar that will give you the lockjaw. Ignorant people think it's the *noise* which fighting cats make that is so aggravating, but it ain't so; it's the sickening grammar they use. Now I've never heard a jay use bad grammar but very seldom; and when they do, they are as ashamed as a human; they shut right down and leave.

"You may call a jay a bird. Well, so he is, in a measure — because he's got feathers on him, and don't belong to no church, perhaps; but otherwise he is just as much a human as you be. And I'll tell you for why. A jay's gifts, and instincts, and feelings, and interests, cover the whole ground. A jay hasn't got any more principle than a congressman. A jay will lie, a jay will steal, a jay will deceive, a jay will betray; and four times out of five, a jay will go back on his solemnest promise. The sacredness of an obligation is a thing which you can't cram into no blue jay's head. Now, on top of all this, there's another thing; a jay can outswear any gentleman in the mines. You think a cat can swear. Well, a cat can; but you give a blue jay a subject that calls for his reserve powers, and where is your cat! Don't talk to me—I know too much about this thing. And there's yet another thing; in the one little particular of scolding—just good, clean, out-and-out scolding—a blue jay can lay over anything, human or divine. Yes, sir, a jay is everything that a man is. A jay can cry, a jay can laugh, a jay can feel shame, a jay can reason and plan and discuss, a jay likes gossip and scandal, a jay has got a sense of humor, a jay knows when he is an ass just as well as you do—maybe better. If a jay ain't human, he better take in his sign, that's all. Now I'm going to tell you a perfectly true fact about some blue jays.

"When I first begun to understand jay language correctly, there was a little incident happened here. Seven years ago, the last man in this region but me moved away. There stands his house—been empty ever since; a log house, with a plank roof—just one big room, and no more; no ceiling—nothing between the rafters and the floor. Well, one Sunday morning I was sitting out here in front of my cabin, with my cat, taking the sun, and looking at the blue hills, and listening to the leaves rustling so lonely in the trees, and thinking of the home away yonder in the states, that I hadn't heard from in thirteen years, when a blue jay lit on that house, with an acorn in his mouth, and says, 'Hello, I reckon I've struck something.' When he spoke, the acorn dropped out of his mouth and rolled down the roof, of course, but he didn't care; his mind was all on the thing he had struck. It was a knothole in the roof. He cocked his head to one side, shut one eye and put the other one to the hole, like a possum looking down a jug; then he glanced up with his bright eyes, gave a wink or two with his wings—which signifies gratification, you understand—and says, 'It looks like a hole, it's located like a hole—blamed if I don't believe it *is* a hole!'

"Then he cocked his head down and took another look; he glances up perfectly joyful, this time; winks his wings and his tail both, and says, 'Oh, no, this ain't no fat thing, I reckon! If I ain't in luck!—Why it's a perfectly elegant hole!' So he flew down and got that acorn, and fetched it up and dropped it in, and was just tilting his head back, with the heavenliest smile on his face, when all of a sudden he was paralyzed into a listening attitude and that smile faded gradually out of his countenance like breath off'n a razor, and the strangest look of surprise took its place. Then he says, 'Why, I didn't hear it fall!' He cocked his eye at the hole again, and took a long look; raised up and shook his head; stepped around to the other side of the hole and took another look from that side; shook his head again. He studied a while, then he just went into the Details—walked round and round the hole and spied into it from every point of the compass. No use. Now he took a thinking attitude on the comb of the roof and scratched the back of his head with his right foot a minute, and finally says, 'Well, it's too many for *me*, that's certain; must be a mighty long hole; however, I ain't got no time to fool around here, I got to "tend to business"; I reckon it's all right—chance it, anyway.'

"So he flew off and fetched another acorn and dropped it in, and tried to flirt his eye to the hole quick enough to see what become of it, but he was too late. He held his eye there as much as a minute; then he raised up and sighed, and says, 'Confound it, I don't seem to understand this thing, no way; however, I'll tackle her again.' He fetched another acorn, and done his level best to see what become of it, but he couldn't. He says, 'Well, I never struck no such a hole as this before; I'm of the opinion it's a totally new kind of a hole.' Then he begun to get mad. He held in for a spell, walking up and down the comb of the roof and shaking his head and muttering to himself; but his feelings got the upper hand of him, presently, and he broke loose and cussed himself black in the face. I never see a bird take on so about a little thing. When he got through he walks to the hole and looks in again for half a minute; then he says, 'Well, you're a long hole, and a deep hole, and a mighty singular hole altogether—but I've started in to fill you, and I'm damned if I *don't* fill you, if it takes a hundred years!'

"And with that, away he went. You never see a bird work so since you was born. The way he hove acorns into that hole for about two hours and a half was one of the most exciting and astonishing spectacles I ever struck. He never stopped to take a look anymore—he just hove 'em in and went for more. Well, at last he could hardly flop his wings, he was so tuckered out. He comes a-dropping down, once more, sweating like an ice pitcher, dropped his acorn in and says, 'Now I guess I've got the bulge on you by this time!' So he bent down for a look. If you'll believe me, when his head come up again he was just pale with rage. He says, 'I've shoveled acorns enough in there to keep the family thirty years, and if I can see a sign of one of 'em I wish I may land in a museum with a belly full of sawdust in two minutes!'

"He just had strength enough to crawl up on to the comb and lean his back agin the chimbly, and then he collected his impressions and begun to free his mind. I see in a second that what I had mistook for profanity in the mines was only just the rudiments, as you may say.

"Another jay was going by, and heard him doing his devotions, and stops to inquire what was up. The sufferer told him the whole circumstance, and says, 'Now yonder's the hole, and if you don't believe me, go and look for yourself.' So this fellow went and looked, and comes back and says, 'How many did you say you put in there?' 'Not any less than two tons,' says the sufferer. The other jay went and looked again. He couldn't seem to make it out, so he raised a yell, and three more jays come. They all examined the hole, they all made the sufferer tell it over again, then they all discussed it, and got off as many leather-headed opinions about it as an average crowd of humans could have done.

"They called in more jays; then more and more, till pretty soon this whole region 'peared to have a blue flush about it. There must have been five thousand of them; and such another jawing and disputing and ripping and cussing, you never heard. Every jay in the whole lot put his eye to the hole and delivered a more chuckle-headed opinion about the mystery than the jay that went there before him. They examined the house all over, too. The door was standing half open, and at last one old jay happened to go and light on it and look in. Of course, that knocked the mystery galley-west in a second. There lay the acorns, scattered all over the floor. He flopped his wings and raised a whoop. 'Come here!' he says, 'Come here, everybody; hang'd if this fool hasn't been trying to fill up a house with acorns!' They all came a-swooping down like a blue cloud, and as each fellow lit on the door and took a glance, the whole absurdity of the contract that that first jay had tackled hit him home and he fell over backward suffocating with laughter, and the next jay took his place and done the same.

"Well, sir, they roosted around here on the housetop and the trees for an hour, and guffawed over that thing like human beings. It ain't any use to tell me a blue jay hasn't got a sense of humor, because I know better. And memory, too. They brought jays here from all over the United States to look down that hole, every summer for three years. Other birds, too. And they could all see the point except an owl that come from Nova Scotia to visit the Yosemite, and he took this thing in on his way back. He said he couldn't see anything funny in it. But then he was a good deal disappointed about Yosemite, too."

THE STORYTELLER

by Saki

It was a hot afternoon, and the railway carriage was correspondingly sultry, and the next stop was at Templecombe, nearly an hour ahead. The occupants of the carriage were a small girl, and a smaller girl, and a small boy. An aunt belonging to the children occupied one corner seat, and the further corner seat on the opposite side was occupied by a bachelor who was a stranger to their party, but the small girls and the small boy emphatically occupied the compartment. Both the aunt and the children were conversational in a limited, persistent way, reminding one of the attentions of a housefly that refuses to be discouraged. Most of the aunt's remarks seemed to begin with "Don't," and nearly all of the children's remarks began with "Why?" The bachelor said nothing out loud. "Don't, Cyril, don't," exclaimed the aunt, as the small boy began smacking the cushions of the seat, producing a cloud of dust at each blow.

"Come and look out of the window," she added.

The child moved reluctantly to the window. "Why are those sheep being driven out of that field?" he asked.

"I expect they are being driven to another field where there is more grass," said the aunt weakly.

"But there is lots of grass in that field," protested the boy; "there's nothing else but grass there. Aunt, there's lots of grass in that field."

"Perhaps the grass in the other field is better," suggested the aunt fatuously.

"Why is it better?" came the swift, inevitable question.

"Oh, look at those cows!" exclaimed the aunt. Nearly every field along the line had contained cows or bullocks, but she spoke as though she were drawing attention to a rarity.

"Why is the grass in the other field better?" persisted Cyril.

The frown on the bachelor's face was deepening to a scowl. He was a hard, unsympathetic man, the aunt decided in her mind. She was utterly unable to come to any satisfactory decision about the grass in the other field.

The smaller girl created a diversion by beginning to recite "On the Road to Mandalay." She only knew the first line, but she put her limited knowledge to the fullest possible use. She repeated the line over and over again in a dreamy but resolute and very audible voice; it seemed to the bachelor as though someone had had a bet with her that she could not repeat the line aloud two thousand times without stopping. Whoever it was who had made the wager was likely to lose his bet.

"Come over here and listen to a story," said the aunt, when the bachelor had looked twice at her and once at the communication cord.

The children moved listlessly towards the aunt's end of the carriage. Evidently her reputation as a storyteller did not rank high in their estimation.

In a low, confidential voice, interrupted at frequent intervals by loud, petulant questionings from her listeners, she began an unenterprising and deplorably uninteresting story about a little girl who was good, and made friends with everyone on account of her goodness, and was finally saved from a mad bull by a number of rescuers who admired her moral character.

"Wouldn't they have saved her if she hadn't been good?" demanded the bigger of the small girls. It was exactly the question that the bachelor had wanted to ask.

"Well, yes," admitted the aunt lamely, "but I don't think they would have run quite so fast to her help if they had not liked her so much."

"It's the stupidest story I've ever heard," said the bigger of the small girls, with immense conviction.

"I didn't listen after the first bit, it was so stupid," said Cyril.

The smaller girl made no actual comment on the story, but she had long ago recommenced a murmured repetition of her favourite line.

"You don't seem to be a success as a storyteller," said the bachelor suddenly from his corner.

The aunt bristled in instant defence at this unexpected attack.

"It's a very difficult thing to tell stories that children can both understand and appreciate," she said stiffly.

"I don't agree with you," said the bachelor.

"Perhaps you would like to tell them a story," was the aunt's retort.

"Tell us a story," demanded the bigger of the small girls.

"Once upon a time," began the bachelor, "there was a little girl called Bertha, who was extraordinarily good."

The children's momentarily aroused interest began at once to flicker; all stories seemed dreadfully alike, no matter who told them.

"She did all that she was told, she was always truthful, she kept her clothes clean, ate milk puddings as though they were jam tarts, learned her lessons perfectly, and was polite in her manners."

"Was she pretty?" asked the bigger of the small girls.

"Not as pretty as any of you," said the bachelor, "but she was horribly good."

There was a wave of reaction in favour of the story; the word horrible in connection with goodness was a novelty that commended itself. It seemed to introduce a ring of truth that was absent from the aunt's tales of infant life.

"She was so good," continued the bachelor, "that she won several medals for goodness, which she always wore, pinned on to her dress. There was a medal for obedience, another medal for punctuality, and a third for good behaviour. They were large metal medals and they clicked against one another as she walked. No other child in the town where she lived had as many as three medals, so everybody knew that she must be an extra good child."

"Horribly good," quoted Cyril.

"Everybody talked about her goodness, and the Prince of the country got to hear about it, and he said that as she was so very good she might be allowed once a week to walk in his park, which was just outside the town. It was a beautiful park, and no children were ever allowed in it, so it was a great honour for Bertha to be allowed to go there."

"Were there any sheep in the park?" demanded Cyril.

"No;" said the bachelor, "there were no sheep."

"Why weren't there any sheep?" came the inevitable question arising out of that answer.

The aunt permitted herself a smile, which might almost have been described as a grin.

"There were no sheep in the park," said the bachelor, "because the Prince's mother had once had a dream that her son would either be killed by a sheep or else by a clock falling on him. For that reason the Prince never kept a sheep in his park or a clock in his palace."

The aunt suppressed a gasp of admiration.

"Was the Prince killed by a sheep or by a clock?" asked Cyril.

"He is still alive, so we can't tell whether the dream will come true," said the bachelor unconcernedly; "anyway, there were no sheep in the park, but there were lots of little pigs running all over the place."

"What colour were they?"

"Black with white faces, white with black spots, black all over, grey with white patches, and some were white all over."

The storyteller paused to let a full idea of the park's treasures sink into the children's imaginations; then he resumed:

"Bertha was rather sorry to find that there were no flowers in the park. She had promised her aunts, with tears in her eyes, that she would not pick any of the kind Prince's flowers, and she had meant to keep her promise, so of course it made her feel silly to find that there were no flowers to pick."

"Why weren't there any flowers?"

"Because the pigs had eaten them all," said the bachelor promptly. "The gardeners had told the Prince that you couldn't have pigs and flowers, so he decided to have pigs and no flowers."

There was a murmur of approval at the excellence of the Prince's decision; so many people would have decided the other way.

"There were lots of other delightful things in the park. There were ponds with gold and blue and green fish in them, and trees with beautiful parrots that said clever things at a moment's notice, and humming birds that hummed all the popular tunes of the day. Bertha walked up and down and enjoyed herself immensely, and thought to herself: 'If I were not so extraordinarily good I should not have been allowed to come into this beautiful park and enjoy all that there is to be seen in it,' and her three medals clinked against one another as she walked and helped to remind her how very good she really was. Just then an enormous wolf came prowling into the park to see if it could catch a fat little pig for its supper."

"What colour was it?" asked the children, amid an immediate quickening of interest.

"Mud-colour all over, with a black tongue and pale grey eyes that gleamed with unspeakable ferocity. The first thing that it saw in the park was Bertha; her pinafore was so spotlessly white and clean that it could be seen from a great distance. Bertha saw the wolf and saw that it was stealing towards her, and she began to wish that she had never been allowed to come into the park. She ran as hard as she could, and the wolf came after her with huge leaps and bounds. She managed to reach a shrubbery of myrtle bushes and she hid herself in one of the thickest of the bushes. The wolf came sniffing among the branches, its black tongue lolling out of its mouth and its pale grey eyes glaring with rage. Bertha was terribly frightened, and thought to herself: 'If I had not been so extraordinarily good I should have been safe in the town at this moment.' However, the scent of the myrtle was so strong that the wolf could not sniff out where Bertha was hiding, and the bushes were so thick that he might have hunted about in them for a long time without catching sight of her, so he thought he might as well go off and catch a little pig instead. Bertha was trembling very much at having the wolf prowling and sniffing so near her, and as she trembled the medal for obedience clinked against the medals for good conduct and punctuality. The wolf was just moving away when he heard the sound of the medals clinking and stopped to listen; they clinked again in a bush quite near him. He dashed into the bush, his pale grey eyes gleaming with ferocity and triumph, and dragged Bertha out and devoured her to the last morsel. All that was left of her were her shoes, bits of clothing, and the three medals for goodness."

"Were any of the little pigs killed?"

"No, they all escaped."

"The story began badly," said the smaller of the small girls, "but it had a beautiful ending."

"It is the most beautiful story that I ever heard," said the bigger of the small girls, with immense decision.

"It is the *only* beautiful story I have ever heard," said Cyril.

A dissentient opinion came from the aunt.

"A most improper story to tell to young children! You have undermined the effect of years of careful teaching."

"At any rate," said the bachelor, collecting his belongings preparatory to leaving the carriage, "I kept them quiet for ten minutes, which was more than you were able to do."

"Unhappy woman!" he observed to himself as he walked down the platform of Templecombe station; "for the next six months or so those children will assail her in public with demands for an improper story!"

THE WHIRLIGIG OF LIFE

by O. Henry

Justice-of-the-Peace Benaja Widdup sat in the door of his office smoking his elder-stem pipe. Halfway to the zenith the Cumberland range rose blue-gray in the afternoon haze. A speckled hen swaggered down the main street of the "settlement," cackling foolishly.

Up the road came a sound of creaking axles, and then a slow cloud of dust, and then a bull-cart bearing Ransie Bilbro and his wife. The cart stopped at the Justice's door, and the two climbed down. Ransie was a narrow six feet of sallow brown skin and yellow hair. The imperturbability of the mountains hung upon him like a suit of armor. The woman was calicoed, angled, snuff-brushed, and weary with unknown desires. Through it all gleamed a faint protest of cheated youth unconscious of its loss.

The Justice of the Peace slipped his feet into his shoes,

for the sake of dignity, and moved to let them enter.

"We-all," said the woman, in a voice like the wind blowing through pine boughs, "wants a divo'ce." She looked at Ransie to see if he noted any flaw or ambiguity or evasion or partiality or self-partisanship in her statement of their business.

"A divo'ce," repeated Ransie, with a solemn nod. "We-all can't git along together nohow. It's lonesome enough fur to live in the mount'ins when a man and a woman keers fur one another. But when she's a-spittin' like a wildcat or a-sullenin' like a hoot-owl in the cabin, a man ain't got no call to live with her."

"When he's a no-'count varmint," said the woman, "without any especial warmth, a-traipsin' along of scalawags and moonshiners and a-layin' on his back pizen 'ith co'n whiskey, and a-pesterin' folks with a pack o' hungry, triflin' houn's to feed!"

"When she keeps a-throwin' skillet lids," came Ransie's antiphony, "and slings b'ilin' water on the best coon-dog in the Cumberlands, and sets herself agin' cookin' a man's victuals, and keeps him awake o' nights accusin' him of a sight of doin's!"

"When he's al'ays a-fightin' the revenues, and gits a hard name in the mount'ins fur a mean man, who's gwine to be able fur to sleep o' nights?"

The Justice of the Peace stirred deliberately to his duties. He placed his one chair and a wooden stool for his petitioners. He opened his book of statutes on the table and scanned the index. Presently he wiped his spectacles and shifted his inkstand.

"The law and the statutes," said he, "air silent on the subjeck of divo'ce as fur as the jurisdiction of this co't air concerned. But, accordin' to equity and the Constitution and the golden rule, it's a bad barg'in that can't run both ways. If a justice of the peace can marry a couple, it's plain that he is bound to be able to divo'ce 'em. This here office will issue a decree of divo'ce and abide by the decision of the Supreme Co't to hold it good."

Ransie Bilbro drew a small tobacco-bag from his trousers pocket. Out of this he shook upon the table a five-dollar note. "Sold a b'arskin and two foxes fur that," he remarked. "It's all the money we got."

"The regular price of a divo'ce in this co't," said the Justice, "air five dollars." He stuffed the bill into the pocket of his homespun vest with a deceptive air of indifference. With much bodily toil and mental travail he wrote the decree upon half a sheet of foolscap, and then copied it upon the other. Ransie Bilbro and his wife listened to his reading of the document that was to give them freedom:

"Know all men by these presents that Ransie Bilbro and his wife, Ariela Bilbro, this day personally appeared before me and promises that hereinafter they will neither love, honor, nor obey each other, neither for better nor worse, being of sound mind and body, and accept summons for divorce according to the peace and dignity of the State. Herein fail not, so help you God. Benaja Widdup, justice of the peace in and for the county of Piedmont, State of Tennessee."

The Justice was about to hand one of the documents to Ransie. The voice of Ariela delayed the transfer. Both men looked at her. Their dull masculinity was confronted by something sudden and unexpected in the woman.

"Judge, don't you give him that air paper yit. 'Tain't all settled, nohow. I got to have my rights first. I got to have my ali-money. 'Tain't no kind of a way to do fur a man to divo'ce his wife 'thout her havin' a cent fur to do with. I'm a-layin' off to be a-goin' up to brother Ed's up on Hogback Mount'in. I'm bound fur to hev a pa'r of shoes and some snuff and things besides. Ef Rance kin affo'd a divo'ce, let him pay me ali-money."

Ransie Bilbro was stricken to dumb perplexity. There had been no previous hint of alimony.

Justice Benaja Widdup felt that the point demanded judicial decision. The authorities were also silent on the subject of alimony. But the woman's feet were bare. The trail to Hogback Mountain was steep and flinty.

"Ariela Bilbro," he asked, in official tones, "how much did you 'low would be good and sufficient ali-money in the case befo' the co't."

"I 'lowed," she answered, "fur the shoes and all, to say five dollars. That ain't much fur ali-money, but I reckon that'll git me to up brother Ed's."

"The amount," said the Justice, "air not onreasonable. Ransie Bilbro, you air ordered by the co't to pay the plaintiff the sum of five dollars befo' the decree of divo'ce air issued."

"I hain't no mo' money," breathed Ransie, heavily. "I done paid you all I had."

"Otherwise," said the Justice, looking severely over his spectacles, "you air in contempt of co't."

"I reckon if you gimme till tomorrow," pleaded the husband, "I mout be able to rake or scrape it up somewhars. I never looked for to be a-payin' no alimoney."

"The case air adjourned," said Benaja Widdup, "till tomorrow, when you-all will present yo'selves and obey the order of the co't. Followin' of which the decrees of divo'ce will be delivered." He sat down in the door and began to loosen a shoestring.

"We mout as well go down to Uncle Ziah's," decided Ransie, "and spend the night." He climbed into the cart on one side, and Ariela climbed in on the other. Obeying the flap of his rope, the little red bull slowly came around on a tack, and the cart crawled away in the nimbus arising from its wheels.

Justice-of-the-peace Benaja Widdup smoked his elder-stem pipe. Late in the afternoon he got his weekly paper, and read it until the twilight dimmed its lines. Then he lit the tallow candle on his table, and read until the moon rose, marking the time for supper. He lived in the double log cabin on the slope near the girdled poplar. Going home to supper he crossed a little branch darkened by a laurel thicket. The dark figure of a man stepped from the laurels and pointed a rifle at his breast. His hat was pulled down low, and something covered most of his face.

"I want yo' money," said the figure, "'thout any talk. I'm gettin' nervous, and my finger's a-wabblin' on this here trigger."

"I've only got f-f-five dollars," said the Justice, producing it from his vest pocket.

"Roll it up," came the order, "and stick it in the end of this here gun-bar'l."

The bill was crisp and new. Even fingers that were clumsy and trembling found little difficulty in making a spill of it and inserting it (this with less ease) into the muzzle of the rifle.

"Now I reckon you kin be goin' along," said the robber.

The Justice lingered not on his way.

The next day came the little red bull, drawing the cart to the office door. Justice Benaja Widdup had his shoes on, for he was expecting the visit. In his presence Ransie Bilbro handed to his wife a five-dollar bill. The official's eye sharply viewed it. It seemed to curl up as though it had been rolled and inserted into the end of a gun-barrel. But the Justice refrained from comment. It is true that other bills might be inclined to curl. He handed each one a decree of divorce. Each stood awkwardly silent, slowly folding the guarantee of freedom. The woman cast a shy glance full of constraint at Ransie.

"I reckon you'll be goin' back up to the cabin," she said, along 'ith the bull-cart. There's bread in the tin box settin' on the shelf. I put the bacon in the b'ilin'-pot to keep the hounds from gittin' it. Don't forget to wind the clock tonight."

"You air a-goin' to your brother Ed's?" asked Ransie, with fine unconcern.

"I was 'lowin' to get along up thar afore night. I ain't sayin' as they'll pester theyselves any to make me welcome, but I hain't nowhar else fur to go. It's a right smart ways, and I reckon I better be goin'. I'll be a-sayin' good-bye, Ranse—that is, if you keer fur to say so."

"I don't know as anybody's a hound dog," said Ransie, in a martyr's voice, "fur to not want to say goodbye—'less you air so anxious to git away that you don't want me to say it."

Ariela was silent. She folded the five-dollar bill and her decree carefully, and placed them in the bosom of her dress. Benaja Widdup watched the money disappear with mournful eyes behind his spectacles.

And then with his next words he achieved rank (as his thoughts ran) with either the great crowd of the world's sympathizers or the little crowd of its great financiers.

"Be kind o' lonesome in the old cabin tonight, Ranse," she said.

Ransie Bilbro stared out at the Cumberlands, clear blue now in the sunlight. He did not look at Ariela.

"I 'low it might be lonesome," he said; "but when folks gits mad and wants a divo'ce, you can't make folks stay."

"There's others wanted a divo'ce," said Ariela, speaking to the wooden stool. "Besides, nobody don't want nobody to stay."

"Nobody never said they didn't."

"Nobody never said they did. I reckon I better start on now to brother Ed's."

"Nobody can't wind that old clock."

"Want me to go back along 'ith you in the cart and wind it fur you, Ranse?"

The mountaineer's countenance was proof against emotion. But he reached out a big hand and enclosed Ariela's thin brown one. Her soul peeped out once through her impassive face, hallowing it.

"Them hounds shan't pester you no more," said Ransie. "I reckon I been mean and low down. You wind that clock, Ariela."

"My heart hit's in that cabin, Ranse," she whispered, "along 'ith you. I ai'nt a-goin' to git mad no more. Le's be startin', Ranse, so's we kin git home by sundown."

Justice-of-the-peace Benaja Widdup interposed as they started for the door, forgetting his presence.

"In the name of the State of Tennessee," he said, "I forbid you-all to be a-defyin' of its laws and statutes. This co't is mo' than willin' and full of joy to see the clouds of discord and misunderstandin' rollin' away from two lovin' hearts, but it air the duty of the co't to p'eserve the morals and integrity of the State. The co't reminds you that you air no longer man and wife, but air divo'ced by regular decree, and as such air not entitled to the benefits and 'purtenances of the mattermonal estate."

Ariela caught Ransie's arm. Did those words mean that she must lose him now when they had just learned the lesson of life?

"But the co't air prepared," went on the Justice, "fur to remove the disabilities set up by the decree of divo'ce. The co't air on hand to perform the solemn ceremony of marri'ge, thus fixin' things up and enablin' the parties in the case to resume the honor'ble and elevatin' state of mattermony which they desires. The fee fur performin' said ceremony will be, in this case, to wit, five dollars."

Ariela caught the gleam of promise in his words. Swiftly her hand went to her bosom. Freely as an alighting dove the bill fluttered to the Justice's table. Her sallow cheek colored as she stood hand in hand with Ransie and listened to the reuniting words.

Ransie helped her into the cart, and climbed in beside her. The little red bull turned once more, and they set out, hand-clasped, for the mountains.

Justice-of-the-peace Benaja Widdup sat in his door and took off his shoes. Once again he fingered the bill tucked down in his vest pocket. Once again he smoked his elder-stem pipe. Once again the speckled hen swaggered down the main street of the "settlement," cackling foolishly.

MY BROTHER HENRY

by J. M. Barrie

At first sight it may not, perhaps, seem appropriate that I should be happy because I have at last had the courage to kill my brother Henry. For some time, however, Henry had been annoying me. Strictly speaking, I never had a brother Henry. It is just fifteen months since I began to acknowledge that there was such a person. It came about in this way:—I have a friend of the name of Fenton, who, like myself, lives in London. About a year and a half ago I was at Fenton's, and he remarked that he had met a man the day before who knew my brother Henry. Not having a brother Henry, I felt that there must be a mistake somewhere; so I suggested that Fenton's friend had gone wrong in the name. My only brother, I pointed out with the suavity of manner that makes me a general favourite, was called Alexander.

"Yes," said Fenton, "but he spoke of Alexander also."

Even this did not convince me that I had a brother Henry, and I asked Fenton the name of his friend. Scudamour was the name, and the gentleman had met my brothers Alexander and Henry some six years previously in Paris. When I heard this I probably frowned; for then I knew who my brother Henry was. Strange though it may seem, I was my own brother Henry. I distinctly remembered meeting this man Scudamour at Paris during the time that Alexander and I were there for a week's pleasure, and quarrelled every day. I explained this to Fenton; and there, for the time being, the matter rested.

I had, however, by no means heard the last of Henry. Several times afterwards I heard from various persons that Scudamour wanted to meet me because he knew my brother Henry. At last we did meet, at a Bohemian supper-party in Furnival's Inn; and, almost as soon as he saw me, Scudamour asked where Henry was now. This was precisely what I feared. I am a man who always looks like a boy. There are few persons of my age in London who retain their boyish appearance as long as I have done; indeed, this is the curse of my life. Though I am approaching the age of thirty, I pass for twenty; and I have observed old gentlemen frown at my precocity when I said a good thing or helped myself to a second glass of wine. There was, therefore, nothing surprising in Scudamour's remark that, when he had the pleasure of meeting Henry, Henry must have been about the age that I had now reached. All would have been well had I explained the real state of affairs to this annoying man; but, unfortunately for myself, I loathe entering upon explanations to anybody about anything. When I ring for my boots and my servant thinks I want a glass of water, I drink the water and remain indoors.

Much, then, did I dread a discussion with Scudamour, his surprise when he heard that I was Henry (my Christian name is Thomas), and his comments on my youthful appearance. Besides, I was at that moment carving a tough fowl; and, as I learned to carve from a handbook, I can make no progress unless I keep muttering to myself, "Cut from A to B, taking care to pass along the line C D, and sever the wing K from the body at the point F." There was no likelihood of my meeting Scudamour again, so the easiest way to get rid of him seemed to be to humour him. I therefore told him that Henry was in India, married, and doing well.

"Remember me to Henry when you write to him," was Scudamour's last remark to me that evening.

A few weeks later someone tapped me on the shoulder in Oxford Street. It was Scudamour. "Heard from Henry?" he asked. I said I had heard by the last mail. "Anything particular in the letter?" I felt it would not do to say there was nothing particular in a letter which had come all the way from India, so I hinted that Henry had had trouble with his wife. By this I meant that her health was bad; but he took it up in another way, and I did not set him right.

"Ah, ah!" he said, shaking his head sagaciously, "I'm sorry to hear that. Poor Henry!"

"Poor old boy!" was all I could think of replying.

"How about the children?" Scudamour asked.

"Oh, the children," I said, with what I thought presence of mind, "are coming to England."

"To stay with Alexander?" he asked; for Alexander is a married man.

My answer was that Alexander was expecting them by the middle of next month; and eventually Scudamour went away muttering "Poor Henry!"

In a month or so we met again.

"No word of Henry's getting leave of absence?" asked Scudamour.

I replied shortly that Henry had gone to live in Bombay, and would not be home for years. He saw that I was brusque, so what does he do but draw me aside for a quiet explanation.

"I suppose," he said, "you are annoyed because I told Fenton that Henry's wife had run away from him. The fact is I did it for your good. You see I happened to make a remark to Fenton about your brother Henry, and he said that there was no such person. Of course I laughed at that, and pointed out not only that I had the pleasure of Henry's acquaintance, but that you and I had a talk about the old fellow every time we met. 'Well,' Fenton said, 'this is a most remarkable thing; for Tom,' meaning you, 'said to me in this very room, sitting in that very chair, that Alexander was his only brother.' I saw that Fenton resented your concealing the existence of your brother Henry from him, so I thought the most friendly thing I could do was to tell him that your reticence was doubtless due to the fact that Henry's private affairs were troubling you. Naturally, in the circumstances, you did not want to talk about Henry."

I shook Scudamour by the hand, telling him that he had acted judiciously; but if I could have stabbed him quietly at that moment I dare say I should have done it. I did not see Scudamour again for a long time, for I took care to keep out of his way; but I heard first from him and then of him. One day he wrote to me saying that his nephew was going to Bombay, and would I be so good as to give the youth an introduction to my brother Henry? He also asked me to dine with him and his nephew. I declined the dinner, but I sent the nephew the required note of introduction to Henry.

The next I heard of Scudamour was from Fenton. "By the way," said Fenton, "Scudamour is in Edinburgh at present."

I trembled, for Edinburgh is where Alexander lives. "What has taken him there?" I asked, with assumed carelessness.

Fenton believed it was business; "but," he added, "Scudamour asked me to tell you that he meant to call on Alexander, as he was anxious to see Henry's children."

A few days afterwards I had a telegram from Alexander, who generally uses this means of communication when he corresponds with me. "Do you know a man, Scudamour? Reply," was what Alexander said. I thought of answering that we had met a man of that name when we were in Paris; but, on the whole, replied boldly: "Know no one of the name of Scudamour."

About two months ago I passed Scudamour in Regent Street, and he did not recognise me. This I could have borne if there had been no more of Henry; but I knew that

Scudamour was now telling everybody about Henry's wife.

By-and-by I got a letter from an old friend of Alexander's, asking me if there was any truth in a report that Alexander was going to Bombay. Soon afterwards Alexander wrote to me to say that he had been told by several persons that I was going to Bombay. In short, I saw that the time had come for killing Henry. So I told Fenton that Henry had died of fever, deeply regretted; and asked him to be sure to tell Scudamour, who had always been interested in the deceased's welfare. The other day Fenton told me that he had communicated the sad intelligence to Scudamour.

"How did he take it?" I asked.

"Well," Fenton said, reluctantly, "he told me that when he was up in Edinburgh he did not get on well with Alexander; but he expressed great curiosity as to Henry's children."

"Ah," I said, "the children were both drowned in the Forth; a sad affair—we can't bear to talk of it." I am not likely to see much of Scudamour again, nor is Alexander. Scudamour now goes about saying that Henry was the only one of us he really liked.

TOBERMORY

by Saki

It was a chill, rain-washed afternoon of a late August day, that indefinite season when partridges are still in security or cold storage, and there is nothing to hunt—unless one is bounded on the north by the Bristol Channel, in which case one may lawfully gallop after fat red stags. Lady Blemley's house party was not bounded on the north by the Bristol Channel, hence there was a full gathering of her guests round the tea-table on this particular afternoon. And, in spite of the blankness of the season and the triteness of the occasion, there was no trace in the company of that fatigued restlessness which means a dread of the pianola and a subdued hankering for auction bridge. The undisguised openmouthed attention of the entire party was fixed on the homely negative personality of Mr. Cornelius Appin. Of all her guests, he was the one who had come to Lady Blemley with the vaguest reputation. Someone had said he was "clever," and he had got his invitation in the moderate expectation, on the part of his hostess, that some portion at least of his cleverness would be contributed to the general entertainment. Until teatime that day she had been unable to discover in what direction, if any, his cleverness lay. He was neither a wit nor a croquet champion, a hypnotic force nor a begetter of amateur theatricals. Neither did his exterior suggest the sort of man in whom women are willing to pardon a generous measure of mental deficiency. He had subsided into mere Mr. Appin, and the Cornelius seemed a piece of transparent baptismal bluff. And now he was claiming to have launched on the world a discovery beside which the invention of gunpowder, of the printing press, and of steam locomotion were inconsiderable trifles. Science had made bewildering strides in many directions during recent decades, but this thing seemed to belong to the domain of miracle rather than to scientific achievement.

"And do you really ask us to believe," Sir Wilfrid was saying, "that you have discovered a means for instructing animals in the art of human speech, and that dear old Tobermory has proved your first successful pupil?"

"It is a problem at which I have worked for the last seventeen years," said Mr. Appin, "but only during the last eight or nine months have I been rewarded with glimmerings of success. Of course I have experimented with thousands of animals, but latterly only with cats, those wonderful creatures which have assimilated themselves so marvellously with our civilization while retaining all their highly developed feral instincts. Here and there among cats one comes across an outstanding superior intellect, just as one does among the ruck of human beings, and when I made the acquaintance of Tobermory a week ago I saw at once that I was in contact with a cat of extraordinary intelligence. I had gone far along the road to success in recent experiments; with Tobermory, as you call him, I have reached the goal."

Mr. Appin concluded his remarkable statement in a voice which he strove to divest of a triumphant inflection. No one said "Rats," though Clovis's lips moved in a monosyllabic contortion which probably invoked those rodents of disbelief.

"And do you mean to say," asked Miss Resker, after a slight pause, "that you have taught Tobermory to say and understand easy sentences of one syllable?"

"My dear Miss Resker," said the wonderworker patiently, "one teaches little children in that piecemeal fashion; when one has once solved the problem of making a beginning with an animal of highly developed intelligence one has no need for those halting methods. Tobermory can speak our language with perfect correctness."

This time Clovis very distinctly said, "Beyond-rats!" Sir Wilfrid was more polite, but equally sceptical.

"Hadn't we better have the cat in and judge for ourselves?" suggested Lady Blemley.

Sir Wilfrid went in search of the animal, and the company settled themselves down to the languid expectation of witnessing some more or less adroit drawing room ventriloquism.

In a minute Sir Wilfrid was back in the room, his face white beneath its tan and his eyes dilated with excitement.

"By Gad, it's true!"

His agitation was unmistakably genuine, and his hearers started forward in a thrill of awakened interest.

Collapsing into an armchair he continued breathlessly: "I found him dozing in the smoking room, and called out to him to come for his tea. He blinked at me in his usual way, and I said, 'Come on, Toby; don't keep us waiting;' and, by Gad! He drawled out in a most horribly natural voice that he'd come when he dashed well pleased! I nearly jumped out of my skin!"

Appin had preached to absolutely incredulous hearers; Sir Wilfrid's statement carried instant conviction. A Babel-like chorus of startled exclamation arose, amid which the scientist sat mutely enjoying the first fruit of his stupendous discovery.

In the midst of the clamour Tobermory entered the room and made his way with velvet tread and studied unconcern across to the group seated round the tea-table.

A sudden hush of awkwardness and constraint fell on the company. Somehow there seemed an element of embarrassment in addressing on equal terms a domestic cat of acknowledged mental ability.

"Will you have some milk, Tobermory?" asked Lady Blemley in a rather strained voice.

"I don't mind if I do," was the response, couched in a tone of even indifference. A shiver of suppressed excitement went through the listeners, and Lady Blemley might be excused for pouring out the saucerful of milk rather unsteadily.

"I'm afraid I've spilt a good deal of it," she said apologetically.

"After all, it's not my Axminster," was Tobermory's rejoinder.

Another silence fell on the group, and then Miss Resker, in her best district-visitor manner, asked if the human language had been difficult to learn. Tobermory looked squarely at her for a moment and then fixed his gaze serenely on the middle distance. It was obvious that boring questions lay outside his scheme of life.

"What do you think of human intelligence?" asked Mavis Pellington lamely.

"Of whose intelligence in particular?" asked Tobermory coldly.

"Oh, well, mine for instance," said Mavis, with a feeble laugh.

"You put me in an embarrassing position," said Tobermory, whose tone and attitude certainly did not suggest a shred of embarrassment. "When your inclusion in this house party was suggested Sir Wilfrid protested that you were the most brainless woman of his acquaintance, and that there was a wide distinction between hospitality and the care of the feeble-minded. Lady Blemley replied that your lack of brainpower was the precise quality which had earned you your invitation, as you were the only person she could think of who might be idiotic enough to buy their old car. You know, the one they call 'The Envy of Sisyphus,' because it goes quite nicely uphill if you push it."

Lady Blemley's protestations would have had greater effect if she had not casually suggested to Mavis only that morning that the car in question would be just the thing for her down at her Devonshire home.

Major Barfield plunged in heavily to effect a diversion.

"How about your carryings-on with the tortoiseshell puss up at the stables, eh?"

The moment he had said it everyone realized the blunder.

"One does not usually discuss these matters in public," said Tobermory frigidly. "From a slight observation of your ways since you've been in this house I should imagine you'd find it inconvenient if I were to shift the conversation on to your own little affairs."

The panic which ensued was not confined to the Major.

"Would you like to go and see if cook has got your dinner ready?" suggested Lady Blemley hurriedly, affecting to ignore the fact that it wanted at least two hours to Tobermory's dinner-time.

"Thanks," said Tobermory, "not quite so soon after my tea. I don't want to die of indigestion."

"Cats have nine lives, you know," said Sir Wilfrid heartily.

"Possibly," answered Tobermory; "but only one liver."

"Adelaide!" said Mrs. Cornett, "do you mean to encourage that cat to go out and gossip about us in the servants' hall?"

The panic had indeed become general. A narrow ornamental balustrade ran in front of most of the bedroom windows at the Towers, and it was recalled with dismay that this had formed a favourite promenade for Tobermory at all hours, where he could watch the pigeons—and heaven knew what else besides. If he intended to become reminiscent in his present outspoken strain the effect would be something more than disconcerting. Mrs. Cornett, who spent much time at her toilet table, and whose complexion was reputed to be of a nomadic though punctual disposition, looked as ill at ease as the Major. Miss Scrawen, who wrote fiercely sensuous poetry and led a blameless life, merely displayed irritation; if you are methodical and virtuous in private you don't necessarily want everyone to know it. Bertie van Tahn, who was so depraved at seventeen that he had long ago given up trying to be any worse, turned a dull shade of gardenia white, but he did not commit the error of dashing out of the room like Odo Finsberry, a young gentleman who was understood to be reading for the Church and who was possibly disturbed at the thought of scandals he might hear concerning other people. Clovis had the presence of mind to maintain a composed exterior; privately he was calculating how long it would take to procure a box of fancy mice as hush money.

Even in a delicate situation like the present, Agnes Resker could not endure to remain too long in the background.

"Why did I ever come down here?" she asked dramatically.

Tobermory immediately accepted the opening.

"Judging by what you said to Mrs. Cornett on the

croquet lawn yesterday, you were out for food. You described the Blemleys as the dullest people to stay with that you knew, but said they were clever enough to employ a first-rate cook; otherwise they'd find it difficult to get anyone to come down a second time."

"There's not a word of truth in it! I appeal to Mrs. Cornett—" exclaimed the discomfited Agnes.

"Mrs. Cornett repeated your remark afterwards to Bertie van Tahn," continued Tobermory, "and said, 'That woman is a regular Hunger Marcher; she'd go anywhere for four square meals a day,' and Bertie van Tahn said—"

At this point the chronicle mercifully ceased. Tobermory had caught a glimpse of the big yellow Tom from the Rectory working his way through the shrubbery towards the stable wing. In a flash he had vanished through the open French window.

With the disappearance of his too brilliant pupil Cornelius Appin found himself beset by a hurricane of bitter upbraiding, anxious inquiry, and frightened entreaty. The responsibility for the situation lay with him, and he must prevent matters from becoming worse. Could Tobermory impart his dangerous gift to other cats? was the first question he had to answer. It was possible, he replied, that he might have initiated his intimate friend the stable puss into his new accomplishment, but it was unlikely that his teaching could have taken a wider range as yet.

"Then," said Mrs. Cornett, "Tobermory may be a valuable cat and a great pet; but I'm sure you'll agree, Adelaide, that both he and the stable cat must be done away with without delay."

"You don't suppose I've enjoyed the last quarter of an hour, do you?" said Lady Blemley bitterly. "My husband and I are very fond of Tobermory—at least, we were before this horrible accomplishment was infused into him; but now, of course, the only thing is to have him destroyed as soon as possible."

"We can put some strychnine in the scraps he always gets at dinner-time," said Sir Wilfrid, "and I will go and drown the stable cat myself. The coachman will be very sore at losing his pet, but I'll say a very catching form of mange has broken out in both cats and we're afraid of it spreading to the kennels."

"But my great discovery!" expostulated Mr. Appin; "after all my years of research and experiment—"

"You can go and experiment on the shorthorns at the farm, who are under proper control," said Mrs. Cornett, "or the elephants at the Zoological Gardens. They're said to be highly intelligent, and they have this recommendation, that they don't come creeping about our bedrooms and under chairs, and so forth."

An archangel ecstatically proclaiming the Millennium, and then finding that it clashed unpardonably with Henley and would have to be indefinitely postponed, could hardly have felt more crestfallen than Cornelius Appin at the reception of his wonderful achievement. Public opinion, however, was against him—in fact, had the general voice been consulted on the subject it is probable that a strong minority vote would have been in favour of including him in the strychnine diet.

Defective train arrangements and a nervous desire to

see matters brought to a finish prevented an immediate dispersal of the party, but dinner that evening was not a social success. Sir Wilfrid had had rather a trying time with the stable cat and subsequently with the coachman. Agnes Resker ostentatiously limited her meal to a morsel of dry toast, which she bit as though it were a personal enemy; while Mavis Pellington maintained a vindictive silence throughout the meal. Lady Blemley kept up a flow of what she hoped was conversation, but her attention was fixed on the doorway. A plateful of carefully dosed fish scraps was in readiness on the sideboard, but sweets and savoury and dessert went their way, and no Tobermory appeared either in the dining room or kitchen.

The sepulchral dinner was cheerful compared with the subsequent vigil in the smoking room. Eating and drinking had at least supplied a distraction and cloak to the prevailing embarrassment. Bridge was out of the question in the general tension of nerves and tempers, and after Odo Finsberry had given a lugubrious rendering of "Melisande in the Wood" to a frigid audience, music was tacitly avoided. At eleven the servants went to bed, announcing that the small window in the pantry had been left open as usual for Tobermory's private use. The guests read steadily through the current batch of magazines. Lady Blemley made periodic visits to the pantry, returning each time with an expression of listless depression which forestalled questioning.

At two o'clock Clovis broke the dominating silence.

"He won't turn up tonight. He's probably in the local newspaper office at the present moment, dictating the first instalment of his reminiscences. Lady What's-her-name's book won't be in it. It will be the event of the day."

Having made this contribution to the general cheerfulness, Clovis went to bed. At long intervals the various members of the house party followed his example.

The servants taking round the early tea made a uniform announcement in reply to a uniform question. Tobermory had not returned.

Breakfast was, if anything, a more unpleasant function than dinner had been, but before its conclusion the situation was relieved. Tobermory's corpse was brought in from the shrubbery, where a gardener had just discovered it. From the bites on his throat and the yellow fur which coated his claws it was evident that he had fallen in unequal combat with the big Tom from the Rectory.

By midday most of the guests had quitted the Towers, and after lunch Lady Blemley had sufficiently recovered her spirits to write an extremely nasty letter to the Rectory about the loss of her valuable pet.

Tobermory had been Appin's one successful pupil, and he was destined to have no successor. A few weeks later an elephant in the Dresden Zoological Garden, which had shown no previous signs of irritability, broke loose and killed an Englishman who had apparently been teasing it. The victim's name was variously reported in the papers as Oppin and Eppelin, but his front name was faithfully rendered Cornelius.

"If he was trying German irregular verbs on the poor beast," said Clovis, "he deserved all he got."

THE CHANGELING

by W. W. Jacobs

Mr. George Henshaw let himself in at the front door, and stood for some time wiping his boots on the mat. The little house was ominously still, and a faint feeling, only partially due to the lapse of time since breakfast, manifested itself behind his waistcoat. He coughed—a matter-of-fact cough—and, with an attempt to hum a tune, hung his hat on the peg and entered the kitchen.

Mrs. Henshaw had just finished dinner. The neatly cleaned bone of a chop was on a plate by her side; a small dish which had contained a rice pudding was empty; and the only food left on the table was a small rind of cheese and a piece of stale bread. Mr. Henshaw's face fell, but he drew his chair up to the table and waited.

His wife regarded him with a fixed and offensive stare. Her face was red and her eyes were blazing. It was hard to ignore her gaze; harder still to meet it. Mr. Henshaw, steering a middle course, allowed his eyes to wander round the room and to dwell, for the fraction of a second, on her angry face.

"You've had dinner early?" he said at last, in a trembling voice.

"Have I?" was the reply.

Mr. Henshaw sought for a comforting explanation. "Clock's fast," he said, rising and adjusting it.

His wife rose almost at the same moment, and with slow deliberate movements began to clear the table.

"What—what about dinner?" said Mr. Henshaw, still trying to control his fears.

"Dinner!" repeated Mrs. Henshaw, in a terrible voice. "You go and tell that creature you were on the bus with to get your dinner."

Mr. Henshaw made a gesture of despair. "I tell you," he said emphatically, "it wasn't me. I told you so last night. You get an idea in your head and—"

"That'll do," said his wife, sharply. "I saw you, George Henshaw, as plain as I see you now. You were tickling her ear with a bit o' straw, and that good-for-nothing friend of yours, Ted Stokes, was sitting behind with another beauty. Nice way o' going on, and me at ' all alone by myself, slaving and slaving to keep things respectable!"

"It wasn't me," reiterated the unfortunate.

"When I called out to you," pursued the unheeding Mrs. Henshaw, "you started and pulled your hat over your eyes and turned away. I should have caught you if it hadn't been for all them carts in the way and falling down. I can't understand now how it was I wasn't killed; I was a mask of mud from head to foot."

Despite his utmost efforts to prevent it, a faint smile flitted across the pallid features of Mr. Henshaw.

"Yes, you may laugh," stormed his wife, "and I've no doubt them two beauties laughed too. I'll take care you don't have much more to laugh at, my man."

She flung out of the room and began to wash up the crockery. Mr. Henshaw, after standing irresolute for some time with his hands in his pockets, put on his hat again and left the house.

He dined badly at a small eating-house, and returned home at six o'clock that evening to find his wife out and the cupboard empty. He went back to the same restaurant for tea, and after a gloomy meal went round to discuss the situation with Ted Stokes. That gentleman's suggestion of a double alibi he thrust aside with disdain and a stern appeal to talk sense.

"Mind, if my wife speaks to you about it," he said, warningly, "it wasn't me, but somebody like me. You might say he 'ad been mistook for me before."

Mr. Stokes grinned and, meeting a freezing glance from his friend, at once became serious again.

"Why not say it was you?" he said stoutly. "There's no harm in going for a 'bus-ride with a friend and a couple o' ladies."

"O' course there ain't," said the other, hotly, "else I shouldn't ha' done it. But you know what my wife is."

Mr. Stokes, who was by no means a favourite of the lady in question, nodded. "You *were* a bit larky, too," he said thoughtfully. "You 'ad quite a little slapping game after you pretended to steal her brooch."

"I s'pose when a gentleman's with a lady he 'as got to make 'imself pleasant?" said Mr. Henshaw, with dignity. "Now, if my missis speaks to you about it, you say that it wasn't me, but a friend of yours up from the country who is as like me as two peas. See?"

"Name o' Dodd," said Mr. Stokes, with a knowing nod. "Tommy Dodd."

"I'm not playing the giddy goat," said the other, bitterly, "and I'd thank you not to."

"All right," said Mr. Stokes, somewhat taken aback. "Any name you like; I don't mind."

Mr. Henshaw pondered. "Any sensible name'll do," he said, stiffly.

"Bell?" suggested Mr. Stokes. "Alfred Bell? I did know a man o' that name once. He tried to borrow a bob off of me."

"That'll do," said his friend, after some consideration; "but mind you stick to the same name. And you'd better make up something about him— where he lives, and all that sort of thing—so that you can stand being questioned without looking more like a silly fool than you can help."

"I'll do what I can for you," said Mr. Stokes, "but I don't s'pose your missis'll come to me at all. She saw you plain enough."

They walked on in silence and, still deep in thought over the matter, turned into a neighbouring tavern for refreshment. Mr. Henshaw drank his with the air of a man performing a duty to his constitution; but Mr. Stokes, smacking his lips, waxed eloquent over the brew.

"I hardly know what I'm drinking," said his friend, forlornly. "I suppose it's four-half, because that's what I asked for."

Mr. Stokes gazed at him in deep sympathy. "It can't be so bad as that," he said, with concern.

"You wait till you're married," said Mr. Henshaw, brusquely. "You'd no business to ask me to go with you, and I was a good-natured fool to do it."

"You stick to your tale and it'll be all right," said the other. "Tell her that you spoke to me about it, and that his name is Alfred Bell—B E double L—and that he lives in— in Ireland. Here! I say!"

"Well," said Mr. Henshaw, shaking off the hand which the other had laid on his arm.

"You—you be Alfred Bell," said Mr. Stokes, breathlessly.

Mr. Henshaw started and eyed him nervously. His friend's eyes were bright and, he fancied, a bit wild.

"Be Alfred Bell," repeated Mr. Stokes. "Don't you see? Pretend to be Alfred Bell and go with me to your missis. I'll lend you a suit o' clothes and a fresh neck-tie, and there you are."

"*What?*" roared the astounded Mr. Henshaw.

"It's as easy as easy," declared the other. "Tomorrow evening, in a new rig-out, I walks you up to your house and asks for you to show you to yourself. Of course, I'm sorry you ain't in, and perhaps we walks in to wait for you."

"Show me to myself?" gasped Mr. Henshaw.

Mr. Stokes winked. "On account o' the surprising

likeness," he said, smiling. "It is surprising, ain't it? Fancy the two of us sitting there and talking to her and waiting for you to come in and wondering what's making you so late!"

Mr. Henshaw regarded him steadfastly for some seconds, and then, taking a firm hold of his mug, slowly drained the contents.

"And what about my voice?" he demanded, with something approaching a sneer.

"That's right," said Mr. Stokes, hotly; "it wouldn't be you if you didn't try to make difficulties."

"But what about it?" said Mr. Henshaw, obstinately.

"You can alter it, can't you?" said the other.

They were alone in the bar, and Mr. Henshaw, after some persuasion, was induced to try a few experiments. He ranged from bass, which hurt his throat, to a falsetto which put Mr. Stokes's teeth on edge, but in vain. The rehearsal was stopped at last by the landlord, who, having twice come into the bar under the impression that fresh customers had entered, spoke his mind at some length. "Seem to think you're in a blessed monkey-house," he concluded, severely.

"We thought we was," said Mr. Stokes, with a long appraising sniff, as he opened the door. "It's a mistake anybody might make."

He pushed Mr. Henshaw into the street as the landlord placed a hand on the flap of the bar, and followed him out.

"You'll have to 'ave a bad cold and talk in 'usky whispers," he said slowly, as they walked along. "You caught a cold travelling in the train from Ireland day before yesterday, and you made it worse going for a ride on the outside of a bus with me and a couple o' ladies. See? Try 'usky whispers now."

Mr. Henshaw tried, and his friend, observing that he was taking but a languid interest in the scheme, was loud in his praises. "I should never 'ave known you," he declared. "Why, it's wonderful! Why didn't you tell me you could act like that?"

Mr. Henshaw remarked modestly that he had not been aware of it himself, and, taking a more hopeful view of the situation, whispered himself into such a state of hoarseness that another visit for refreshment became absolutely necessary.

"Keep your 'art up and practise," said Mr. Stokes, as he shook hands with him some time later. "And if you can manage it, get off at four o'clock tomorrow and we'll go round to see her while she thinks you're still at work."

Mr. Henshaw complimented him upon his artfulness, and, with some confidence in a man of such resource, walked home in a more cheerful frame of mind. His heart sank as he reached the house, but to his relief the lights were out and his wife was in bed.

He was up early next morning, but his wife showed no signs of rising. The cupboard was still empty, and for some time he moved about hungry and undecided. Finally he mounted the stairs again, and with a view to arranging matters for the evening remonstrated with her upon her behaviour and loudly announced his intention of not coming home until she was in a better frame of mind. From a disciplinary point of view the effect of the remonstrance was somewhat lost by being shouted through the closed door, and he also broke off too abruptly when Mrs. Henshaw opened it suddenly and confronted him. Fragments of the peroration reached her through the front door.

Despite the fact that he left two hours earlier, the day passed but slowly, and he was in a very despondent state of mind by the time he reached Mr. Stokes's lodging. The latter, however, had cheerfulness enough for both, and, after helping his visitor to change into fresh clothes and part his hair in the middle instead of at the side, surveyed him with grinning satisfaction. Under his directions Mr. Henshaw also darkened his eyebrows and beard with a little burnt cork until Mr. Stokes declared that his own mother wouldn't know him.

"Now, be careful," said Mr. Stokes, as they set off. "Be bright and cheerful; be a sort o' ladies' man to her, same as she saw you with the one on the 'bus. Be as unlike yourself as you can, and don't forget yourself and call her by 'er pet name."

"Pet name!" said Mr. Henshaw, indignantly. "Pet name! You'll alter your ideas of married life when you're caught, my lad, I can tell you!"

He walked on in scornful silence, lagging farther and farther behind as they neared his house. When Mr. Stokes knocked at the door he stood modestly aside with his back against the wall of the next house.

"Is George in?" inquired Mr. Stokes, carelessly, as Mrs. Henshaw opened the door.

"No," was the reply.

Mr. Stokes affected to ponder; Mr. Henshaw instinctively edged away.

"He ain't in," said Mrs. Henshaw, preparing to close the door.

"I wanted to see 'im partikler," said Mr. Stokes, slowly. "I brought a friend o' mine, name o' Alfred Bell, up here on purpose to see 'im."

Mrs. Henshaw, following the direction of his eyes, put her head round the door.

"George!" she exclaimed, sharply.

Mr. Stokes smiled. "That ain't George," he said, gleefully; "That's my friend, Mr. Alfred Bell. Ain't it a extraordinary likeness? Ain't it wonderful? That's why I brought 'im up; I wanted George to see 'im."

Mrs. Henshaw looked from one to the other in wrathful bewilderment.

"His living image, ain't he?" said Mr. Stokes. "This is my pal George's missis," he added, turning to Mr. Bell.

"Good afternoon to you," said that gentleman, huskily.

"He got a bad cold coming from Ireland," explained Mr. Stokes, "and, foolish-like, he went outside a bus with me the other night and made it worse."

"Oh-h!" said Mrs. Henshaw, slowly. "Indeed! Really!"

"He's quite curious to see George," said Mr. Stokes. "In fact, he was going back to Ireland tonight if it 'adn't been for that. He's waiting till tomorrow just to see George."

Mr. Bell, in a voice huskier than ever, said that he had altered his mind again.

"Nonsense!" said Mr. Stokes, sternly. "Besides, George would like to see you. I s'pose he won't be long?" he added, turning to Mrs. Henshaw, who was regarding Mr. Bell much as a hungry cat regards a plump sparrow.

"I don't suppose so," she said, slowly.

"I dare say if we wait a little while—" began Mr. Stokes, ignoring a frantic glance from Mr. Henshaw.

"Come in," said Mrs. Henshaw, suddenly.

Mr. Stokes entered and, finding that his friend hung back, went out again and half led, half pushed him indoors. Mr. Bell's shyness he attributed to his having lived so long in Ireland.

"He is quite the ladies' man, though," he said, artfully, as they followed their hostess into the front room. "You should ha' seen 'im the other night on the bus. We had a couple o' lady friends o' mine with us, and even the conductor was surprised at his goings on."

Mr. Bell, by no means easy as to the results of the experiment, scowled at him despairingly.

"Carrying on, was he?" said Mrs. Henshaw, regarding the culprit steadily.

"Carrying on like one o'clock," said the imaginative Mr. Stokes. "Called one of 'em his little wife, and asked her where 'er wedding ring was."

"I didn't," said Mr. Bell, in a suffocating voice. "I didn't."

"There's nothing to be ashamed of," said Mr. Stokes, virtuously. "Only, as I said to you at the time, 'Alfred,' I says, 'it's all right for you as a single man, but you might be the twin brother of a pal o' mine— George Henshaw by name—and if some people was to see you they might think it was 'im.' Didn't I say that?"

"You did," said Mr. Bell, helplessly.

"And he wouldn't believe me," said Mr. Stokes, turning to Mrs. Henshaw. "That's why I brought him round to see George."

"I should like to see the two of 'em together myself," said Mrs. Henshaw, quietly. "I should have taken him for my husband anywhere."

"You wouldn't if you'd seen 'im last night," said Mr. Stokes, shaking his head and smiling.

"Carrying on again, was he?" inquired Mrs. Henshaw, quickly.

"No!" said Mr. Bell, in a stentorian whisper.

His glance was so fierce that Mr. Stokes almost quailed. "I won't tell tales out of school," he said, nodding.

"Not if I ask you to?" said Mrs. Henshaw, with a winning smile.

"Ask 'im," said Mr. Stokes.

"Last night," said the whisperer, hastily, "I went for a quiet walk round Victoria Park all by myself. Then I met Mr. Stokes, and we had one half-pint together at a public house. That's all."

Mrs. Henshaw looked at Mr. Stokes. Mr. Stokes winked at her.

"It's as true as my name is—Alfred Bell," said that gentleman, with slight but natural hesitation.

"Have it your own way," said Mr. Stokes, somewhat perturbed at Mr. Bell's refusal to live up to the character he had arranged for him.

"I wish my husband spent his evenings in the same quiet way," said Mrs. Henshaw, shaking her head.

"Don't he?" said Mr. Stokes. "Why, he always seems quiet enough to me. Too quiet, I should say. Why, I never knew a quieter man. I chaff 'im about it sometimes."

"That's his artfulness," said Mrs. Henshaw.

"Always in a hurry to get 'ome," pursued the benevolent Mr. Stokes.

"He may say so to you to get away from you," said Mrs. Henshaw, thoughtfully. "He does say you're hard to shake off sometimes."

Mr. Stokes sat stiffly upright and threw a fierce glance in the direction of Mr. Henshaw.

"Pity he didn't tell me," he said bitterly. "I ain't one to force my company where it ain't wanted."

"I've said to him sometimes," continued Mrs. Henshaw, "'Why don't you tell Ted Stokes plain that you don't like his company?' but he won't. That ain't his way. He'd sooner talk of you behind your back."

"What does he say?" inquired Mr. Stokes, coldly ignoring a frantic headshake on the part of his friend.

"Promise me you won't tell him if I tell you," said Mrs. Henshaw.

Mr. Stokes promised.

"I don't know that I ought to tell you," said Mrs. Henshaw, reluctantly, "but I get so sick and tired of him coming home and grumbling about you."

"Go on," said the waiting Stokes.

Mrs. Henshaw stole a glance at him. "He says you act as if you thought yourself everybody," she said, softly, "and your everlasting clack, clack, clack, worries him to death."

"Go on," said the listener, grimly.

"And he says it's so much trouble to get you to pay for your share of the drinks that he'd sooner pay himself and have done with it."

Mr. Stokes sprang from his chair and, with clenched fists, stood angrily regarding the horrified Mr. Bell. He composed himself by an effort and resumed his seat.

"Anything else?" he inquired.

"Heaps and heaps of things," said Mrs. Henshaw; "but I don't want to make bad blood between you."

"Don't mind me," said Mr. Stokes, glancing balefully over at his agitated friend. "P'raps I'll tell you some things about him some day."

"It would be only fair," said Mrs. Henshaw, quickly. "Tell me now; I don't mind Mr. Bell hearing; not a bit."

Mr. Bell spoke up for himself. "I don't want to hear family secrets," he whispered, with an imploring glance at the vindictive Mr. Stokes. "It wouldn't be right."

"Well, *I* don't want to say things behind a man's back," said the latter, recovering himself. "Let's wait till George comes in, and I'll say 'em before his face."

Mrs. Henshaw, biting her lip with annoyance, argued with him, but in vain. Mr. Stokes was firm, and, with a glance at the clock, said that George would be in soon and he would wait till he came.

Conversation flagged despite the efforts of Mrs. Henshaw to draw Mr. Bell out on the subject of Ireland. At an early stage of the catechism he lost his voice entirely, and thereafter sat silent while Mrs. Henshaw discussed the most intimate affairs of her husband's family with Mr. Stokes. She was in the middle of an anecdote about her mother-in-law when Mr. Bell rose and, with some difficulty, intimated his desire to depart.

"What, without seeing George?" said Mrs. Henshaw. "He can't be long now, and I should like to see you together."

"P'r'aps we shall meet him," said Mr. Stokes, who was getting rather tired of the affair. "Good night."

He led the way to the door and, followed by the eager Mr. Bell, passed out into the street. The knowledge that Mrs. Henshaw was watching him from the door kept him silent until they had turned the corner, and then, turning fiercely on Mr. Henshaw, he demanded to know what he meant by it.

"I've done with you," he said, waving aside the other's denials. "I've got you out of this mess, and now I've done with you. It's no good talking, because I don't want to hear it."

"Goodbye, then," said Mr. Henshaw, with unexpected hauteur, as he came to a standstill.

"I'll 'ave my trousers first, though," said Mr. Stokes, coldly, "and then you can go, and welcome."

"It's my opinion she recognized me, and said all that just to try us," said the other, gloomily.

Mr. Stokes scorned to reply, and reaching his lodging stood by in silence while the other changed his clothes. He refused Mr. Henshaw's hand with a gesture he had once seen on the stage, and, showing him downstairs, closed the door behind him with a bang.

Left to himself, the small remnants of Mr. Henshaw's courage disappeared. He wandered forlornly up and down the streets until past ten o'clock, and then, cold and dispirited, set off in the direction of home. At the corner of the street he pulled himself together by a great effort, and walking rapidly to his house put the key in the lock and turned it.

The door was locked and the lights were out. He knocked, at first lightly, but gradually increasing in loudness. At the fourth knock a light appeared in the room above, the window was raised, and Mrs. Henshaw leaned out

"*Mr. Bell!*" she said, in tones of severe surprise.

"*Bell?*" said her husband, in a more surprised voice still. "It's me, Polly."

"Go away at once, sir!" said Mrs. Henshaw, indignantly. "How dare you call me by my Christian name? I'm surprised at you!"

"It's me, I tell you—George!" said her husband, desperately. "What do you mean by calling me Bell?"

"If you're Mr. Bell, as I suppose, you know well enough," said Mrs. Henshaw, leaning out and regarding him fixedly; "and if you're George you don't."

"I'm George," said Mr. Henshaw, hastily.

"I'm sure I don't know what to make of it," said Mrs. Henshaw, with a bewildered air. "Ted Stokes brought round a man named Bell this afternoon so like you that I can't tell the difference. I don't know what to do, but I do know this—I don't let you in until I have seen you both together, so that I can tell which is which."

"Both together!" exclaimed the startled Mr. Henshaw. "Here—look here!"

He struck a match and, holding it before his face, looked up at the window. Mrs. Henshaw scrutinized him gravely.

"It's no good," she said, despairingly. "I can't tell. I must see you both together."

Mr. Henshaw ground his teeth. "But where is he?" he inquired.

"He went off with Ted Stokes," said his wife. "If you're George you'd better go and ask him."

She prepared to close the window, but Mr. Henshaw's voice arrested her.

"And suppose he is not there?" he said.

Mrs. Henshaw reflected. "If he is not there bring Ted Stokes back with you," she said at last, "and if he says you're George, I'll let you in." The window closed and the light disappeared. Mr. Henshaw waited for some time, but in vain, and, with a very clear idea of the reception he would meet with at the hands of Mr. Stokes, set off to his lodging.

If anything, he had underestimated his friend's powers. Mr. Stokes, rudely disturbed just as he had got into bed, was the incarnation of wrath. He was violent, bitter, and insulting in a breath, but Mr. Henshaw was desperate, and Mr. Stokes, after vowing over and over again that nothing should induce him to accompany him back to his house, was at last so moved by his entreaties that he went upstairs and equipped himself for the journey.

"And, mind, after this I never want to see your face again," he said, as they walked swiftly back.

Mr. Henshaw made no reply. The events of the day had almost exhausted him, and silence was maintained until they reached the house. Much to his relief he heard somebody moving about upstairs after the first knock, and in a very short time the window was gently raised and Mrs. Henshaw looked out.

"What, you've come back?" she said, in a low, intense voice. "Well, of all the impudence! How dare you carry on like this?"

"It's me," said her husband.

"Yes, I see it is," was the reply.

"It's him right enough; it's your husband," said Mr. Stokes. "Alfred Bell has gone."

"How dare you stand there and tell me them falsehoods!" exclaimed Mrs. Henshaw. "I wonder the ground don't open and swallow you up. It's Mr. Bell, and if he don't go away I'll call the police."

Messrs. Henshaw and Stokes, amazed at their reception, stood blinking up at her. Then they conferred in whispers.

"If you can't tell 'em apart, how do you know this is Mr. Bell?" inquired Mr. Stokes, turning to the window again.

"How do I know?" repeated Mrs. Henshaw. "How do I know? Why, because my husband came home almost directly after Mr. Bell had gone. I wonder he didn't meet him."

"Came home?" cried Mr. Henshaw, shrilly. "*Came home*?"

"Yes; and don't make so much noise," said Mrs. Henshaw, tartly; "he's asleep."

The two gentlemen turned and gazed at each other in stupefaction. Mr. Stokes was the first to recover, and, taking his dazed friend by the arm, led him gently away. At the end of the street he took a deep breath, and, after a slight pause to collect his scattered energies, summed up the situation.

"She's twigged it all along," he said, with conviction. "You'll have to come home with me tonight, and tomorrow the best thing you can do is to make a clean breast of it. It was a silly game, and, if you remember, I was against it from the first."

SELF-MADE MEN

by Stephen Leacock

They were both what we commonly call successful businessmen—men with well-fed faces, heavy signet rings on fingers like sausages, and broad, comfortable waistcoats, a yard and a half round the equator. They were seated opposite each other at a table of a first-class restaurant, and had fallen into conversation while waiting to give their order to the waiter. Their talk had drifted back to their early days and how each had made his start in life when he first struck New York.

"I tell you what, Jones," one of them was saying, "I shall never forget my first few years in this town. By George, it was pretty uphill work! Do you know, sir, when I first struck this place, I hadn't more than fifteen cents to my name, hadn't a rag except what I stood up in, and all the place I had to sleep in—you won't believe it, but it's a gospel fact just the same—was an empty tar barrel. No, sir," he went on, leaning back and closing up his eyes into an expression of infinite experience, "no, sir, a fellow accustomed to luxury like you has simply no idea what sleeping out in a tar barrel and all that kind of thing is like."

"My dear Robinson," the other man rejoined briskly, "if you imagine I've had no experience of hardship of that sort, you never made a bigger mistake in your life. Why, when I first walked into this town I hadn't a cent, sir, not a cent, and as for lodging, all the place I had for months and months was an old piano box up a lane, behind a factory. Talk about hardship, I guess I had it pretty rough! You take a fellow that's used to a good warm tar barrel and put him into a piano box for a night or two, and you'll see mighty soon—"

"My dear fellow," Robinson broke in with some irritation, "you merely show that you don't know what a tar barrel's like. Why, on winter nights, when you'd be shut in there in your piano box just as snug as you please, I used to lie awake shivering, with the draught fairly running in at the bunghole at the back."

"Draught!" sneered the other man, with a provoking laugh, "draught! Don't talk to me about draughts. This box I speak of had a whole darned plank off it, right on the north side too. I used to sit there studying in the evenings, and the snow would blow in a foot deep. And yet, sir," he continued more quietly, "though I know you'll not believe it, I don't mind admitting that some of the happiest days of my life were spent in that same old box. Ah, those were good old times! Bright, innocent days, I can tell you. I'd wake up there in the mornings and fairly shout with high spirits. Of course, you may not be able to stand that kind of life—"

"Not stand it!" cried Robinson fiercely; "me not stand it! By gad! I'm made for it. I just wish I had a taste of the old life again for a while. And as for innocence! Well, I'll bet you you weren't one-tenth as innocent as I was; no, nor one-fifth, nor one-third! What a grand old life it was! You'll swear this is a darned lie and refuse to believe it—but I can remember evenings when I'd have two or three fellows in, and we'd sit round and play pedro by a candle half the night."

"Two or three!" laughed Jones; "why, my dear fellow, I've known half a dozen of us to sit down to supper in my piano box, and have a game of pedro afterwards; yes, and charades and forfeits, and every other darned thing. Mighty good suppers they were too! By Jove, Robinson, you fellows round this town who have ruined your digestions with high living, have no notion of the zest with which a man can sit down to a few potato peelings, or a bit of broken pie crust, or—"

"Talk about hard food," interrupted the other, "I guess I know all about that. Many's the time I've breakfasted off a little cold porridge that somebody was going to throw away from a back door, or that I've gone round to a livery stable and begged a little bran mash that they intended for the pigs. I'll venture to say I've eaten more hog's food—"

"Hog's food!" shouted Robinson, striking his fist savagely on the table, "I tell you hog's food suits me better than—"

He stopped speaking with a sudden grunt of surprise as the waiter appeared with the question:

"What may I bring you for dinner, gentlemen?"

"Dinner!" said Jones, after a moment of silence, "dinner! Oh, anything, nothing—I never care what I eat—give me a little cold porridge, if you've got it, or a chunk of salt pork—anything you like, it's all the same to me."

The waiter turned with an impassive face to Robinson.

"You can bring me some of that cold porridge too," he said, with a defiant look at Jones; "yesterday's, if you have it, and a few potato peelings and a glass of skim milk."

There was a pause. Jones sat back in his chair and looked hard across at Robinson. For some moments the two men gazed into each other's eyes with a stern, defiant intensity. Then Robinson turned slowly round in his seat and beckoned to the waiter, who was moving off with the muttered order on his lips.

"Here, waiter," he said with a savage scowl, "I guess I'll change that order a little. Instead of that cold porridge I'll take—um, yes—a little hot partridge. And you might as well bring me an oyster or two on the half shell, and a mouthful of soup (mock-turtle, consommé, anything), and perhaps you might fetch along a dab of fish, and a little peck of Stilton, and a grape, or a walnut."

The waiter turned to Jones.

"I guess I'll take the same," he said simply, and added; "and you might bring a quart of champagne at the same time."

And nowadays, when Jones and Robinson meet, the memory of the tar barrel and the piano box is buried as far out of sight as a home for the blind under a landslide.

THE CANTERVILLE GHOST

by Oscar Wilde

When Mr. Hiram B. Otis, the American Minister, bought Canterville Chase, everyone told him he was doing a very foolish thing, as there was no doubt at all that the place was haunted. Indeed, Lord Canterville himself, who was a man of the most punctilious honour, had felt it his duty to mention the fact to Mr. Otis when they came to discuss terms.

"We have not cared to live in the place ourselves," said Lord Canterville, "since my grandaunt, the Dowager Duchess of Bolton, was frightened into a fit, from which she never really recovered, by two skeleton hands being placed on her shoulders as she was dressing for dinner, and I feel bound to tell you, Mr. Otis, that the ghost has been seen by several living members of my family, as well as by the rector of the parish, the Rev. Augustus Dampier, who is a Fellow of King's College, Cambridge. After the unfortunate accident to the Duchess, none of our younger servants would stay with us, and Lady Canterville often got very little sleep at night, in consequence of the mysterious noises that came from the corridor and the library."

"My Lord," answered the Minister, "I will take the furniture and the ghost at a valuation. I have come from a modern country, where we have everything that money can buy; and with all our spry young fellows painting the Old World red, and carrying off your best actors and prima-donnas, I reckon that if there were such a thing as a ghost in Europe, we'd have it at home in a very short time in one of our public museums, or on the road as a show."

"I fear that the ghost exists," said Lord Canterville, smiling, "though it may have resisted the overtures of your enterprising impresarios. It has been well known for three centuries, since 1584 in fact, and always makes its appearance before the death of any member of our family."

"Well, so does the family doctor for that matter, Lord Canterville. But there is no such thing, sir, as a ghost, and I guess the laws of Nature are not going to be suspended for the British aristocracy."

"You are certainly very natural in America," answered Lord Canterville, who did not quite understand Mr. Otis's last observation, "and if you don't mind a ghost in the house, it is all right. Only you must remember I warned you."

A few weeks after this, the purchase was concluded, and at the close of the season the Minister and his family went down to Canterville Chase. Mrs. Otis, who, as Miss Lucretia R. Tappan, of West 53d Street, had been a celebrated New York belle, was now a very handsome, middle-aged woman, with fine eyes, and a superb profile. Many American ladies on leaving their native land adopt an appearance of chronic ill health, under the impression that it is a form of European refinement, but Mrs. Otis had never fallen into this error. She had a magnificent constitution, and a really wonderful amount of animal spirits. Her eldest son, christened Washington by his parents in a moment of patriotism, which he never ceased to regret, was a fair-haired, rather good-looking young man, who had qualified himself for American diplomacy by leading the German at the Newport Casino for three successive seasons, and even in London was well known as an excellent dancer. Gardenias and the peerage were his only weaknesses. Otherwise he was extremely sensible. Miss Virginia E. Otis was a little girl of fifteen, lithe and lovely as a fawn, and with a fine freedom in her large blue eyes. She was a wonderful Amazon, and had once raced old Lord Bilton on her pony twice round the park, winning by a length and a half, just in front of the Achilles statue, to the huge delight of the young Duke of Cheshire, who proposed for her on the spot, and was sent back to Eton that very night by his guardians, in floods of tears. After Virginia came the twins, who were usually called "The Star and Stripes," as they were always getting caned. They were delightful boys, and, with the exception of the worthy Minister, the only true republicans of the family.

As Canterville Chase is seven miles from Ascot, the

nearest railway station, Mr. Otis had telegraphed for a waggonette to meet them, and they started on their drive in high spirits. It was a lovely July evening, and the air was delicate with the scent of the pinewoods. Now and then they heard a wood-pigeon brooding over its own sweet voice, or saw, deep in the rustling fern, the burnished breast of the pheasant. Little squirrels peered at them from the beech trees as they went by, and the rabbits scudded away through the brushwood and over the mossy knolls, with their white tails in the air. As they entered the avenue of Canterville Chase, however, the sky became suddenly overcast with clouds, a curious stillness seemed to hold the atmosphere, a great flight of rooks passed silently over their heads, and, before they reached the house, some big drops of rain had fallen.

Standing on the steps to receive them was an old woman, neatly dressed in black silk, with a white cap and apron. This was Mrs. Umney, the housekeeper, whom Mrs. Otis, at Lady Canterville's earnest request, had consented to keep in her former position. She made them each a low curtsey as they alighted, and said in a quaint, old-fashioned manner, "I bid you welcome to Canterville Chase." Following her, they passed through the fine Tudor hall into the library, a long, low room, panelled in black oak, at the end of which was a large stained glass window. Here they found tea laid out for them, and, after taking off their wraps, they sat down and began to look round, while Mrs. Umney waited on them.

Suddenly Mrs. Otis caught sight of a dull red stain on the floor just by the fireplace, and, quite unconscious of what it really signified, said to Mrs. Umney, "I am afraid something has been spilt there."

"Yes, madam," replied the old housekeeper in a low voice, "blood has been spilt on that spot."

"How horrid!" cried Mrs. Otis; "I don't at all care for bloodstains in a sitting room. It must be removed at once."

The old woman smiled, and answered in the same low, mysterious voice, "It is the blood of Lady Eleanore de Canterville, who was murdered on that very spot by her own husband, Sir Simon de Canterville, in 1575. Sir Simon survived her nine years, and disappeared suddenly under very mysterious circumstances. His body has never been discovered, but his guilty spirit still haunts the Chase. The bloodstain has been much admired by tourists and others, and cannot be removed."

"That is all nonsense," cried Washington Otis; "Pinkerton's Champion Stain Remover and Paragon Detergent will clean it up in no time," and before the terrified housekeeper could interfere, he had fallen upon his knees, and was rapidly scouring the floor with a small stick of what looked like a black cosmetic. In a few moments no trace of the bloodstain could be seen.

"I knew Pinkerton would do it," he exclaimed, triumphantly, as he looked round at his admiring family; but no sooner had he said these words than a terrible flash of lightning lit up the sombre room, a fearful peal of thunder made them all start to their feet, and Mrs. Umney fainted.

"What a monstrous climate!" said the American Minister, calmly, as he lit a long cheroot. "I guess the old country is so overpopulated that they have not enough decent weather for everybody. I have always been of opinion that emigration is the only thing for England."

"My dear Hiram," cried Mrs. Otis, "what can we do with a woman who faints?"

"Charge it to her like breakages," answered the Minister; "she won't faint after that;" and in a few moments Mrs. Umney certainly came to. There was no doubt, however, that she was extremely upset, and she sternly warned Mr. Otis to beware of some trouble coming to the house.

"I have seen things with my own eyes, sir," she said, "that would make any Christian's hair stand on end, and many and many a night I have not closed my eyes in sleep for the awful things that are done here." Mr. Otis, however, and his wife warmly assured the honest soul that they were not afraid of ghosts, and, after invoking the blessings of Providence on her new master and mistress, and making arrangements for an increase of salary, the old housekeeper tottered off to her own room.

II

The storm raged fiercely all that night, but nothing of particular note occurred. The next morning, however, when they came down to breakfast, they found the terrible stain of blood once again on the floor. "I don't think it can be the fault of the Paragon Detergent," said Washington, "for I have tried it with everything. It must be the ghost." He accordingly rubbed out the stain a second time, but the second morning it appeared again. The third morning also it was there, though the library had been locked up at night by Mr. Otis himself, and the key carried upstairs. The whole family were now quite interested; Mr. Otis began to suspect that he had been too dogmatic in his denial of the existence of ghosts, Mrs. Otis expressed her intention of joining the Psychical Society, and Washington prepared a long letter to Messrs. Myers and Podmore on the subject of the Permanence of Sanguineous Stains when connected with Crime. That night all doubts about the objective existence of phantasmata were removed forever.

The day had been warm and sunny; and, in the cool of the evening, the whole family went out to drive. They did not return home till nine o'clock, when they had a light supper. The conversation in no way turned upon ghosts, so there were not even those primary conditions of receptive expectations which so often precede the presentation of psychical phenomena. The subjects discussed, as I have since learned from Mr. Otis, were merely such as form the ordinary conversation of cultured Americans of the better class, such as the immense superiority of Miss Fanny Devonport over Sarah Bernhardt as an actress; the difficulty of obtaining green corn, buckwheat cakes, and hominy, even in the best English houses; the importance of Boston in the development of the world-soul; the advantages of the baggage-check system in railway travelling; and the sweetness of the New York accent as compared to the London drawl. No mention at all was made of the supernatural, nor was Sir Simon de Canterville alluded to in any way. At eleven o'clock the family retired, and by half-past all the lights were out. Some time after, Mr. Otis was awakened by a curious noise in the corridor, outside his room. It sounded like the clank of metal, and seemed to be coming nearer every moment. He got up at once, struck a match, and looked at the time. It was exactly one o'clock. He was quite calm, and felt his pulse, which was not at all feverish. The strange noise still continued, and with it he heard distinctly the sound of footsteps. He put on his slippers, took a small oblong phial out of his dressing-case, and opened the door. Right in front of him he saw, in the wan moonlight, an old man of terrible aspect. His eyes were as red burning coals; long grey hair fell over his shoulders in matted coils; his garments, which were of antique cut, were soiled and ragged, and from his wrists and ankles hung heavy manacles and rusty gyves.

"My dear sir," said Mr. Otis, "I really must insist on your oiling those chains, and have brought you for that purpose a small bottle of the Tammany Rising Sun Lubricator. It is said to be completely efficacious upon one application, and there are several testimonials to that effect on the wrapper from some of our most eminent native divines. I shall leave it here for you by the bedroom candles, and will be happy to supply you with more, should you require it." With these words the United States Minister laid the bottle down on a marble table, and, closing his door, retired to rest.

For a moment the Canterville ghost stood quite motionless in natural indignation; then, dashing the bottle violently upon the polished floor, he fled down the corridor, uttering hollow groans, and emitting a ghastly green light. Just, however, as he reached the top of the great oak staircase, a door was flung open, two little white-robed figures appeared, and a large pillow whizzed past his head! There was evidently no time to be lost, so, hastily adopting the Fourth dimension of Space as a means of escape, he vanished through the wainscoting, and the house became quite quiet.

On reaching a small secret chamber in the left wing, he leaned up against a moonbeam to recover his breath, and began to try and realize his position. Never, in a brilliant and uninterrupted career of three hundred years, had he been so grossly insulted. He thought of the Dowager Duchess, whom he had frightened into a fit as she stood before the glass in her lace and diamonds; of the four housemaids, who had gone into hysterics when he merely grinned at them through the curtains on one of the spare bedrooms; of the rector of the parish, whose candle he had blown out as he was coming late one night from the library, and who had been under the care of Sir William Gull ever since, a perfect martyr to nervous disorders; and of old Madame de Tremouillac, who, having wakened up one morning early and seen a skeleton seated in an armchair by the fire reading her diary, had been confined to her bed for six weeks with an attack of brain fever, and, on her recovery, had become reconciled to the Church, and broken off her connection with that notorious sceptic, Monsieur de Voltaire. He remembered the terrible night when the wicked Lord Canterville was found choking in his dressing-room, with the knave of diamonds halfway down his throat, and confessed, just before he died, that he had cheated Charles James Fox out of £50,000 at Crockford's by means of that very card, and swore that the ghost had made him swallow it. All his great achievements came back to him again, from the butler who had shot himself in the pantry because he had seen a green hand tapping at the window pane, to the beautiful Lady Stutfield, who was always obliged to wear a black velvet band round her throat to hide the mark of five fingers burnt upon her white skin, and who drowned herself at last in the carp pond at the end of the King's Walk. With the enthusiastic egotism of the true artist, he went over his most celebrated performances, and smiled bitterly to himself as he recalled to mind his last appearance as "Red Reuben, or the Strangled Babe," his *début* as "Guant Gibeon, the Bloodsucker of Bexley Moor," and the *furore* he had excited one lovely June evening by merely playing ninepins with his own bones upon the lawn-tennis ground. And after all this some wretched modern Americans were to come and offer him the Rising Sun Lubricator, and throw pillows at his head! It was quite unbearable. Besides, no ghost in history had ever been treated in this manner. Accordingly, he determined to have vengeance, and remained till daylight in an attitude of deep thought.

III

The next morning, when the Otis family met at breakfast, they discussed the ghost at some length. The

United States Minister was naturally a little annoyed to find that his present had not been accepted. "I have no wish," he said, "to do the ghost any personal injury, and I must say that, considering the length of time he has been in the house, I don't think it is at all polite to throw pillows at him,"—a very just remark, at which, I am sorry to say, the twins burst into shouts of laughter. "Upon the other hand," he continued, "if he really declines to use the Rising Sun Lubricator, we shall have to take his chains from him. It would be quite impossible to sleep, with such a noise going on outside the bedrooms."

For the rest of the week, however, they were undisturbed, the only thing that excited any attention being the continual renewal of the bloodstain on the library floor. This certainly was very strange, as the door was always locked at night by Mr. Otis, and the windows kept closely barred. The chameleon-like colour, also, of the stain excited a good deal of comment. Some mornings it was a dull (almost Indian) red, then it would be vermilion, then a rich purple, and once when they came down for family prayers, according to the simple rites of the Free American Reformed Episcopalian Church, they found it a bright emerald-green. These kaleidoscopic changes naturally amused the party very much, and bets on the subject were freely made every evening. The only person who did not enter into the joke was little Virginia, who, for some unexplained reason, was always a good deal distressed at the sight of the bloodstain, and very nearly cried the morning it was emerald-green.

The second appearance of the ghost was on Sunday

night. Shortly after they had gone to bed they were suddenly alarmed by a fearful crash in the hall. Rushing downstairs, they found that a large suit of old armour had become detached from its stand, and had fallen on the stone floor, while seated in a high-backed chair was the Canterville ghost, rubbing his knees with an expression of acute agony on his face. The twins, having brought their pea-shooters with them, at once discharged two pellets on him, with that accuracy of aim which can only be attained by long and careful practice on a writing-master, while the United States Minister covered him with his revolver, and called upon him, in accordance with Californian etiquette, to hold up his hands! The ghost started up with a wild shriek of rage, and swept through them like a mist, extinguishing Washington Otis's candle as he passed, and so leaving them all in total darkness. On reaching the top of the staircase he recovered himself, and determined to give his celebrated peal of demoniac laughter. This he had on more than one occasion found extremely useful. It was said to have turned Lord Raker's wig grey in a single night, and had certainly made three of Lady Canterville's French governesses give warning before their month was up. He accordingly laughed his most horrible laugh, till the old vaulted roof rang and rang again, but hardly had the fearful echo died away when a door opened, and Mrs. Otis came out in a light blue dressing-gown. "I am afraid you are far from well," she said, "and have brought you a bottle of Doctor Dobell's tincture. If it is indigestion, you will find it a most excellent remedy." The ghost glared at her in fury, and began at once to make preparations for turning himself into a large black dog, an accomplishment for which he was justly renowned, and to which the family doctor always attributed the permanent idiocy of Lord Canterville's uncle, the Hon. Thomas Horton. The sound of approaching footsteps, however, made him hesitate in his fell purpose, so he contented himself with becoming faintly phosphorescent, and vanished with a deep churchyard groan, just as the twins had come up to him.

On reaching his room he entirely broke down, and became a prey to the most violent agitation. The vulgarity of the twins, and the gross materialism of Mrs. Otis, were naturally extremely annoying, but what really distressed him most was that he had been unable to wear the suit of mail. He had hoped that even modern Americans would be thrilled by the sight of a spectre in armour, if for no more sensible reason, at least out of respect for their natural poet Longfellow, over whose graceful and attractive poetry he himself had while away many a weary hour when the Cantervilles were up in town. Besides it was his own suit. He had worn it with great success at the Kenilworth tournament, and had been highly complimented on it by no less a person than the Virgin Queen herself. Yet when he had put it on, he had been completely overpowered by the weight of the huge breastplate and steel casque, and had fallen heavily on the stone pavement, barking both his knees severely, and bruising the knuckles of his right hand.

For some days after this he was extremely ill, and hardly stirred out of his room at all, except to keep the bloodstain in proper repair. However, by taking great care of himself, he recovered, and resolved to make a third attempt to frighten the United States Minister and his family. He selected Friday, August 17th, for his appearance, and spent most of that day in looking over his wardrobe, ultimately deciding in favour of a large slouched hat with a red feather, a winding-sheet frilled at the wrists and neck, and a rusty dagger. Towards evening a violent storm of rain came on, and the wind was so high that all the windows and doors in the old house shook and rattled. In fact, it was just such weather as he loved. His plan of action was this. He was to make his way quietly to Washington Otis's room, gibber at him from the foot of the bed, and stab himself three times in the throat to the sound of low music. He bore Washington a special grudge, being quite aware that it was he who was in the habit of removing the famous Canterville bloodstain by means of Pinkerton's Paragon Detergent. Having reduced the reckless and foolhardy youth to a condition of abject terror, he was then to proceed to the room occupied by the United States Minister and his wife, and there to place a clammy hand on Mrs. Otis's forehead, while he hissed into her trembling husband's ear the awful secrets of the charnel-house. With regard to little Virginia, he had not quite made up his mind. She had never insulted him in any way, and was pretty and gentle. A few hollow groans from the wardrobe, he thought, would be more than sufficient, or, if that failed to wake her, he might grabble at the counterpane with palsy-twitching fingers. As for the twins, he was quite determined to teach them a lesson. The first thing to be done was, of course, to sit upon their chests, so as to produce the stifling sensation of nightmare. Then, as their beds were quite close to each other, to stand between them in the form of a green, icy-cold corpse, till they became paralyzed with fear, and finally, to throw off the winding-sheet, and crawl round the room, with white, bleached bones and one rolling eyeball, in the character of "Dumb Daniel, or the Suicide's Skeleton," a *role* in which he had on more than one occasion produced a great effect, and which he considered quite equal to his famous part of "Martin the Maniac, or the Masked Mystery."

At half-past ten he heard the family going to bed. For some time he was disturbed by wild shrieks of laughter from the twins, who, with the light-hearted gaiety of schoolboys, were evidently amusing themselves before they retired to rest, but at a quarter-past eleven all was still, and, as midnight sounded, he sallied forth. The owl beat against the window panes, the raven croaked from the old yew tree, and the wind wandered moaning round the house like a lost soul; but the Otis family slept unconscious of their doom, and high above the rain and storm he could hear the steady snoring of the Minister for the United States. He stepped stealthily out of the wainscoting, with an evil smile on his cruel, wrinkled mouth, and the moon hid her face in a cloud as he stole past the great oriel window, where his own arms and those of his murdered wife were blazoned in azure and gold. On and on he glided, like an evil shadow, the very darkness seeming to loathe him as he passed. Once he thought he heard something call, and stopped; but it was only the baying of a dog from the Red Farm, and he went on, muttering strange sixteenth-century curses, and ever and anon brandishing the rusty dagger in the midnight air. Finally he reached the corner of the passage that led to luckless Washington's room. For a moment he paused there, the wind blowing his long grey locks about his head, and twisting into grotesque and fantastic folds the nameless horror of the dead man's shroud. Then the clock struck the quarter, and he felt the time was come. He chuckled to himself, and turned the corner; but no sooner had he done so than, with a piteous wail of terror, he fell back, and hid his blanched face in his long, bony hands. Right in front of him was standing a horrible spectre, motionless as a carven image, and monstrous as a madman's dream! Its head was bald and burnished; its face round, and fat, and white; and hideous laughter seemed to have writhed its features into an eternal grin. From the eyes streamed rays of scarlet light, the mouth was a wide well of fire, and a hideous garment, like his own, swathed with its silent snows the Titan form. On its breast was a placard with strange writing in antique characters, some scroll of shame it seemed, some record of wild sins, some awful calendar of crime, and, with its right hand, it bore aloft a falchion of gleaming steel.

Never having seen a ghost before, he naturally was terribly frightened, and, after a second hasty glance at the awful phantom, he fled back to his room, tripping up in his long winding-sheet as he sped down the corridor, and finally dropping the rusty dagger into the Minister's jackboots, where it was found in the morning by the butler. Once in the privacy of his own apartment, he flung himself down on a small pallet-bed, and hid his face under the clothes. After a time, however, the brave old Canterville spirit asserted itself, and he determined to go and speak to the other ghost as soon as it was daylight. Accordingly, just as the dawn was touching the hills with silver, he returned towards the spot where he had first laid eyes on the grisly phantom, feeling that, after all, two ghosts were better than one, and that, by the aid of his new friend, he might safely grapple with the twins. On reaching the spot, however, a terrible sight met his gaze. Something had evidently happened to the spectre, for the light had entirely faded from its hollow eyes, the gleaming falchion had fallen from its hand, and it was leaning up against the wall in a strained and uncomfortable attitude. He rushed forward and seized it in his arms, when, to his horror, the head slipped off and rolled on the floor, the body assumed a recumbent posture, and he found himself clasping a white dimity bed-curtain, with a sweeping brush, a kitchen cleaver, and a hollow turnip lying at his feet! Unable to understand this curious transformation, he clutched the placard with feverish haste, and there, in the grey morning light, he read these fearful words:—

YE OTIS GHOSTE
Ye Onlie True and Originale Spook,
Beware of Ye Imitationes.
All others are counterfeite.

The whole thing flashed across him. He had been tricked, foiled, and outwitted! The old Canterville look came into his eyes; he ground his toothless gums together;

and, raising his withered hands high above his head, swore according to the picturesque phraseology of the antique school, that, when Chanticleer had sounded twice his merry horn, deeds of blood would be wrought, and murder walk abroad with silent feet.

Hardly had he finished this awful oath when, from the red-tiled roof of a distant homestead, a cock crew. He laughed a long, low, bitter laugh, and waited. Hour after hour he waited, but the cock, for some strange reason, did not crow again. Finally, at half-past seven, the arrival of the housemaids made him give up his fearful vigil, and he stalked back to his room, thinking of his vain oath and baffled purpose. There he consulted several books of ancient chivalry, of which he was exceedingly fond, and found that, on every occasion on which this oath had been used, Chanticleer had always crowed a second time. "Perdition seize the naughty fowl," he muttered, "I have seen the day when, with my stout spear, I would have run him through the gorge, and made him crow for me an 'twere in death!" He then retired to a comfortable lead coffin, and stayed there till evening.

IV

The next day the ghost was very weak and tired. The terrible excitement of the last four weeks was beginning to have its effect. His nerves were completely shattered, and he started at the slightest noise. For five days he kept his room, and at last made up his mind to give up the point of the bloodstain on the library floor. If the Otis family did not want it, they clearly did not deserve it. They were evidently people on a low, material plane of existence, and quite incapable of appreciating the symbolic value of sensuous phenomena. The question of phantasmic apparitions, and the development of astral bodies, was of course quite a different matter, and really not under his control. It was his solemn duty to appear in the corridor once a week, and to gibber from the large oriel window on the first and third Wednesdays in every month, and he did not see how he could honourably escape from his obligations. It is quite true that his life had been very evil, but, upon the other hand, he was most conscientious in all things connected with the supernatural. For the next three Saturdays, accordingly, he traversed the corridor as usual between midnight and three o'clock, taking every possible precaution against being either heard or seen. He removed his boots, trod as lightly as possible on the old worm-eaten boards, wore a large black velvet cloak, and was careful to use the Rising Sun Lubricator for oiling his chains. I am bound to acknowledge that it was with a good deal of difficulty that he brought himself to adopt this last mode of protection. However, one night, while the family were at dinner, he slipped into Mr. Otis's bedroom and carried off the bottle. He felt a little humiliated at first, but afterwards was sensible enough to see that there was a great deal to be said for the invention, and, to a certain degree, it served his purpose. Still in spite of everything he was not left unmolested. Strings were continually being stretched across the corridor, over which he tripped in the dark, and on one occasion, while dressed for the part of

"Black Isaac, or the Huntsman of Hogley Woods," he met with a severe fall, through treading on a butter-slide, which the twins had constructed from the entrance of the Tapestry Chamber to the top of the oak staircase. This last insult so enraged him, that he resolved to make one final effort to assert his dignity and social position, and determined to visit the insolent young Etonians the next night in his celebrated character of "Reckless Rupert, or the Headless Earl."

He had not appeared in this disguise for more than seventy years; in fact, not since he had so frightened pretty Lady Barbara Modish by means of it, that she suddenly broke off her engagement with the present Lord Canterville's grandfather, and ran away to Gretna Green with handsome Jack Castletown, declaring that nothing in the world would induce her to marry into a family that allowed such a horrible phantom to walk up and down the terrace at twilight. Poor Jack was afterwards shot in a duel by Lord Canterville on Wandsworth Common, and Lady Barbara died of a broken heart at Tunbridge Wells before the year was out, so, in every way, it had been a great success. It was, however an extremely difficult "make-up," if I may use such a theatrical expression in connection with one of the greatest mysteries of the supernatural, or, to employ a more scientific term, the higher-natural world, and it took him fully three hours to make his preparations. At last everything was ready, and he was very pleased with his appearance. The big leather riding boots that went with the dress were just a little too large for him, and he could only find one of the two horse-pistols, but, on the whole, he was quite satisfied, and at a quarter-past one he glided out of the wainscoting and crept down the corridor. On reaching the room occupied by the twins, which I should mention was called the Blue Bed Chamber, on account of the colour of its hangings, he found the door just ajar. Wishing to make an effective entrance, he flung it wide open, when a heavy jug of water fell right down on him, wetting him to the skin, and just missing his left shoulder by a couple of inches. At the same moment he heard stifled shrieks of laughter proceeding from the four-post bed. The shock to his nervous system was so great that he fled back to his room as hard as he could go, and the next day he was laid up with a severe cold. The only thing that at all consoled him in the whole affair was the fact that he had not brought his head with him, for, had he done so, the consequences might have been very serious.

He now gave up all hope of ever frightening this rude American family, and contented himself, as a rule, with creeping about the passages in list slippers, with a thick red muffler round his throat for fear of draughts, and a small arquebuse, in case he should be attacked by the twins. The final blow he received occurred on the 19th of September. He had gone downstairs to the great entrance hall, feeling sure that there, at any rate, he would be quite unmolested, and was amusing himself by making satirical remarks on the large Saroni photographs of the United States Minister and his wife which had now taken the place of the Canterville family pictures. He was simply but neatly clad in a long shroud, spotted with churchyard mould, had tied up his jaw with a strip of yellow linen, and carried a small lantern and a sexton's spade. In fact, he was dressed for the character of "Jonas the Graveless, or the Corpse-Snatcher of Chertsey Barn," one of his most remarkable impersonations, and one which the Cantervilles had every reason to remember, as it was the real origin of their quarrel with their neighbour, Lord Rufford. It was about a quarter-past two o'clock in the morning, and, as far as he could ascertain, no one was stirring. As he was strolling towards the library, however, to see if there were any traces left of the bloodstain, suddenly there leaped out on him from a dark corner two figures, who waved their arms wildly above their heads, and shrieked out "BOO!" in his ear.

Seized with a panic, which, under the circumstances, was only natural, he rushed for the staircase, but found Washington Otis waiting for him there with the big garden-syringe, and being thus hemmed in by his enemies on every side, and driven almost to bay, he vanished into the great iron stove, which, fortunately for him, was not lit, and had to make his way home through the flues and chimneys, arriving at his own room in a terrible state of dirt, disorder, and despair.

After this he was not seen again on any nocturnal expedition. The twins lay in wait for him on several occasions, and strewed the passages with nutshells every night to the great annoyance of their parents and the servants, but it was of no avail. It was quite evident that his feelings were so wounded that he would not appear. Mr. Otis consequently resumed his great work on the history of the Democratic Party, on which he had been engaged for some years; Mrs. Otis organized a wonderful clam-bake, which amazed the whole county; the boys took to lacrosse euchre, poker, and other American national games, and Virginia rode about the lanes on her pony, accompanied by the young Duke of Cheshire, who had come to spend the last week of his holidays at Canterville Chase. It was generally assumed that the ghost had gone away, and, in fact, Mr. Otis wrote a letter to that effect to Lord Canterville, who, in reply, expressed his great pleasure at the news, and sent his best congratulations to the Minister's worthy wife.

The Otises, however, were deceived, for the ghost was still in the house, and though now almost an invalid, was by no means ready to let matters rest, particularly as he heard that among the guests was the young Duke of Cheshire, whose grand-uncle, Lord Francis Stilton, had once bet a hundred guineas with Colonel Carbury that he would play dice with the Canterville ghost, and was found the next morning lying on the floor of the card room in such a helpless paralytic state that, though he lived on to a great age, he was never able to say anything again but "Double Sixes." The story was well known at the time, though, of course, out of respect to the feelings of the two noble families, every attempt was made to hush it up, and a full account of all the circumstances connected with it will be found in the third volume of Lord Tattle's *Recollections of the Prince Regent and his Friends*. The ghost, then, was naturally very anxious to show that he had not lost his influence over the Stiltons, with whom, indeed, he was distantly connected, his own first cousin having been married *en secondes noces* to the Sieur de Bulkeley, from whom, as everyone knows, the Dukes of Cheshire are lineally descended. Accordingly, he made arrangements for appearing to Virginia's little lover in his celebrated impersonation of "The Vampire Monk, or the Bloodless Benedictine," a performance so horrible that when old Lady Startup saw it, which she did on one fatal New Year's Eve, in the year 1764, she went off into the most piercing shrieks, which culminated in violent apoplexy, and died in three days, after disinheriting the Cantervilles, who were her nearest relations, and leaving all her money to her London apothecary. At the last moment, however, his terror of the twins prevented his leaving his room, and the little Duke slept in peace under the great feathered canopy in the Royal Bedchamber, and dreamed of Virginia.

V

A few days after this, Virginia and her curly-haired cavalier went out riding on Brockley meadows, where she tore her habit so badly in getting through a hedge that, on their return home, she made up her mind to go up by the back staircase so as not to be seen. As she was running past the Tapestry Chamber, the door of which happened to be open, she fancied she saw someone inside, and thinking it was her mother's maid, who sometimes used to bring her work there, looked in to ask her to mend her habit. To her immense surprise, however, it was the Canterville Ghost himself! He was sitting by the window, watching the ruined gold of the yellowing trees fly through the air, and the red leaves dancing madly down the long avenue. His head was leaning on his hand, and his whole attitude was one of extreme depression. Indeed, so forlorn, and so much out of repair did he look, that little Virginia, whose first idea had been to run away and lock herself in her room, was filled with pity, and determined to try and comfort him. So light was her footfall, and so deep his melancholy, that he was not aware of her presence till she spoke to him.

"I am so sorry for you," she said, "but my brothers are going back to Eton tomorrow, and then, if you behave yourself, no one will annoy you."

"It is absurd asking me to behave myself," he answered, looking round in astonishment at the pretty little girl who had ventured to address him, "quite absurd. I must rattle my chains, and groan through keyholes, and walk about at night, if that is what you mean. It is my only reason for existing."

"It is no reason at all for existing, and you know you have been very wicked. Mrs. Umney told us, the first day we arrived here, that you had killed your wife."

"Well, I quite admit it," said the Ghost, petulantly, "but it was a purely family matter, and concerned no one else."

"It is very wrong to kill anyone," said Virginia, who at times had a sweet puritan gravity, caught from some old New England ancestor.

"Oh, I hate the cheap severity of abstract ethics! My wife was very plain, never had my ruffs properly starched, and knew nothing about cookery. Why, there was a buck I had shot in Hogley Woods, a magnificent pricket, and do you know how she had it sent to table? However, it is no matter now, for it is all over, and I don't think it was very nice of her brothers to starve me to death, though I did kill her."

"Starve you to death? Oh, Mr. Ghost—I mean Sir Simon, are you hungry? I have a sandwich in my case. Would you like it?"

"No, thank you, I never eat anything now; but it is very kind of you, all the same, and you are much nicer than the rest of your horrid, rude, vulgar, dishonest family."

"Stop!" cried Virginia, stamping her foot, "it is you who are rude, and horrid, and vulgar, and as for dishonesty, you know you stole the paints out of my box to try and furbish up that ridiculous bloodstain in the library. First you took all my reds, including the vermilion, and I couldn't do any more sunsets, then you took the emerald-green and the chrome-yellow, and finally I had nothing left but indigo and Chinese white, and could only do moonlight scenes, which are always depressing to look at, and not at all easy to paint. I never told on you, though I was very much annoyed, and it was most ridiculous, the whole thing; for who ever heard of emerald-green blood?"

"Well, really," said the Ghost, rather meekly, "what was I to do? It is a very difficult thing to get real blood nowadays, and, as your brother began it all with his Paragon Detergent, I certainly saw no reason why I should not have your paints. As for colour, that is always a matter of taste: the Cantervilles have blue blood, for instance, the very bluest in England; but I know you Americans don't care for things of this kind."

"You know nothing about it, and the best thing you can

do is to emigrate and improve your mind. My father will be only too happy to give you a free passage, and though there is a heavy duty on spirits of every kind, there will be no difficulty about the Custom House, as the officers are all Democrats. Once in New York, you are sure to be a great success. I know lots of people there who would give a hundred thousand dollars to have a grandfather, and much more than that to have a family ghost."

"I don't think I should like America."

"I suppose because we have no ruins and no curiosities," said Virginia, satirically.

"No ruins! No curiosities!" answered the Ghost; "you have your navy and your manners."

"Good evening; I will go and ask papa to get the twins an extra week's holiday."

"Please don't go, Miss Virginia," he cried; "I am so lonely and so unhappy, and I really don't know what to do. I want to go to sleep and I cannot."

"That's quite absurd! You have merely to go to bed and blow out the candle. It is very difficult sometimes to keep awake, especially at church, but there is no difficulty at all about sleeping. Why, even babies know how to do that, and they are not very clever."

"I have not slept for three hundred years," he said sadly, and Virginia's beautiful blue eyes opened in wonder; "for three hundred years I have not slept, and I am so tired."

Virginia grew quite grave, and her little lips trembled like rose leaves. She came towards him, and kneeling down at his side, looked up into his old withered face.

"Poor, poor Ghost," she murmured; "have you no place where you can sleep?"

"Far away beyond the pine woods," he answered, in a low, dreamy voice, "there is a little garden. There the grass grows long and deep, there are the great white stars of the hemlock flower, there the nightingale sings all night long. All night long he sings, and the cold crystal moon looks down, and the yew tree spreads out its giant arms over the sleepers."

Virginia's eyes grew dim with tears, and she hid her face in her hands.

"You mean the Garden of Death," she whispered.

"Yes, death. Death must be so beautiful. To lie in the soft brown earth, with the grasses waving above one's head, and listen to silence. To have no yesterday, and no tomorrow. To forget time, to forget life, to be at peace. You can help me. You can open for me the portals of death's house, for love is always with you, and love is stronger than death is."

Virginia trembled, a cold shudder ran through her, and for a few moments there was silence. She felt as if she was in a terrible dream.

Then the ghost spoke again, and his voice sounded like the sighing of the wind.

"Have you ever read the old prophecy on the library window?"

"Oh, often," cried the little girl, looking up; "I know it quite well. It is painted in curious black letters, and is difficult to read. There are only six lines:

'When a golden girl can win

Prayer from out the lips of sin,
When the barren almond bears,
And a little child gives away its tears,
Then shall all the house be still
And peace come to Canterville.'
But I don't know what they mean."

"They mean," he said, sadly, "that you must weep with me for my sins, because I have no tears, and pray with me for my soul, because I have no faith, and then, if you have always been sweet, and good, and gentle, the angel of death will have mercy on me. You will see fearful shapes in darkness, and wicked voices will whisper in your ear, but they will not harm you, for against the purity of a little child the powers of Hell cannot prevail."

Virginia made no answer, and the ghost wrung his hands in wild despair as he looked down at her bowed golden head. Suddenly she stood up, very pale, and with a strange light in her eyes. "I am not afraid," she said firmly, "and I will ask the angel to have mercy on you."

He rose from his seat with a faint cry of joy, and taking her hand bent over it with old-fashioned grace and kissed it. His fingers were as cold as ice, and his lips burned like fire, but Virginia did not falter, as he led her across the dusky room. On the faded green tapestry were broidered little huntsmen. They blew their tasselled horns and with their tiny hands waved to her to go back. "Go back! Little Virginia," they cried, "go back!" but the ghost clutched her hand more tightly, and she shut her eyes against them. Horrible animals with lizard tails and goggle eyes blinked at her from the carven chimneypiece, and murmured,

"Beware! Little Virginia, beware! We may never see you again," but the Ghost glided on more swiftly, and Virginia did not listen. When they reached the end of the room he stopped, and muttered some words she could not understand. She opened her eyes, and saw the wall slowly fading away like a mist, and a great black cavern in front of her. A bitter cold wind swept round them, and she felt something pulling at her dress. "Quick, quick," cried the Ghost, "or it will be too late," and in a moment the wainscoting had closed behind them, and the Tapestry Chamber was empty.

VI

About ten minutes later, the bell rang for tea, and, as Virginia did not come down, Mrs. Otis sent up one of the footmen to tell her. After a little time he returned and said that he could not find Miss Virginia anywhere. As she was in the habit of going out to the garden every evening to get flowers for the dinner table, Mrs. Otis was not at all alarmed at first, but when six o'clock struck, and Virginia did not appear, she became really agitated, and sent the boys out to look for her, while she herself and Mr. Otis searched every room in the house. At half-past six the boys came back and said that they could find no trace of their sister anywhere. They were all now in the greatest state of excitement, and did not know what to do, when Mr. Otis suddenly remembered that, some few days before, he had given a band of gipsies permission to camp in the park. He accordingly at once set off for Blackfell Hollow, where he knew they were, accompanied by his eldest son and two of the farm servants. The little Duke of Cheshire, who was perfectly frantic with anxiety, begged hard to be allowed to go too, but Mr. Otis would not allow him, as he was afraid there might be a scuffle. On arriving at the spot, however, he found that the gipsies had gone, and it was evident that their departure had been rather sudden, as the fire was still burning, and some plates were lying on the grass. Having sent off Washington and the two men to scour the district, he ran home, and despatched telegrams to all the police inspectors in the county, telling them to look out for a little girl who had been kidnapped by tramps or gipsies. He then ordered his horse to be brought round, and, after insisting on his wife and the three boys sitting down to dinner, rode off down the Ascot road with a groom. He had hardly, however, gone a couple of miles, when he heard somebody galloping after him, and, looking round, saw the little Duke coming up on his pony, with his face very flushed, and no hat. "I'm awfully sorry, Mr. Otis," gasped out the boy, "but I can't eat any dinner as long as Virginia is lost. Please don't be angry with me; if you had let us be engaged last year, there would never have been all this trouble. You won't send me back, will you? I can't go! I won't go!"

The Minister could not help smiling at the handsome young scapegrace, and was a good deal touched at his devotion to Virginia, so leaning down from his horse, he patted him kindly on the shoulders, and said, "Well, Cecil, if you won't go back, I suppose you must come with me, but I must get you a hat at Ascot."

"Oh, bother my hat! I want Virginia!" cried the little Duke, laughing, and they galloped on to the railway station. There Mr. Otis inquired of the stationmaster if anyone answering to the description of Virginia had been seen on the platform, but could get no news of her. The stationmaster, however, wired up and down the line, and assured him that a strict watch would be kept for her, and, after having bought a hat for the little Duke from a linen-draper, who was just putting up his shutters, Mr. Otis rode off to Bexley, a village about four miles away, which he was told was a well-known haunt of the gipsies, as there was a large common next to it. Here they roused up the rural policeman, but could get no information from him, and, after riding all over the common, they turned their horses' heads homewards, and reached the Chase about eleven o'clock, dead-tired and almost heartbroken. They found Washington and the twins waiting for them at the gatehouse with lanterns, as the avenue was very dark. Not the slightest trace of Virginia had been discovered. The gipsies had been caught on Brockley meadows, but she was not with them, and they had explained their sudden departure by saying that they had mistaken the date of Chorton Fair, and had gone off in a hurry for fear they should be late. Indeed, they had been quite distressed at hearing of Virginia's disappearance, as they were very grateful to Mr. Otis for having allowed them to camp in his park, and four of their number had stayed behind to help in the search. The carp pond had been dragged, and the whole Chase thoroughly gone over, but without any result. It was evident that, for that night at any rate, Virginia was lost to them; and it was in a state of the deepest depression that Mr. Otis and the boys walked up to the house, the groom following behind with the two horses and the pony. In the hall they found a group of frightened servants, and lying on a sofa in the library was poor Mrs. Otis, almost out of her mind with terror and anxiety, and having her forehead bathed with eau de cologne by the old housekeeper. Mr. Otis at once insisted on her having something to eat, and ordered up supper for the whole party. It was a melancholy meal, as hardly anyone spoke, and even the twins were awestruck and subdued, as they were very fond of their sister. When they had finished, Mr. Otis, in spite of the entreaties of the little Duke, ordered them all to bed, saying that nothing more could be done that night, and that he would telegraph in the morning to Scotland Yard for some detectives to be sent down immediately. Just as they were passing out of the dining room, midnight began to boom from the clock tower, and when the last stroke sounded they heard a crash and a sudden shrill cry; a dreadful peal of thunder shook the house, a strain of unearthly music floated through the air, a panel at the top of the staircase flew back with a loud noise, and out on the landing, looking very pale and white, with a little casket in her hand, stepped Virginia. In a moment they had all rushed up to her. Mrs. Otis clasped her passionately in her arms, the Duke smothered her with violent kisses, and the twins executed a wild war dance round the group.

"Good heavens! Child, where have you been?" said Mr. Otis, rather angrily, thinking that she had been playing some foolish trick on them. "Cecil and I have been riding all over the country looking for you, and your mother has been frightened to death. You must never play these practical jokes anymore."

"Except on the Ghost! Except on the Ghost!" shrieked the twins, as they capered about.

"My own darling, thank God you are found; you must never leave my side again," murmured Mrs. Otis, as she kissed the trembling child, and smoothed the tangled gold of her hair.

"Papa," said Virginia, quietly, "I have been with the Ghost. He is dead, and you must come and see him. He had been very wicked, but he was really sorry for all that he had done, and he gave me this box of beautiful jewels before he died."

The whole family gazed at her in mute amazement, but she was quite grave and serious; and, turning round, she led them through the opening in the wainscoting down a narrow secret corridor, Washington following with a lighted candle, which he had caught up from the table. Finally, they came to a great oak door, studded with rusty nails. When Virginia touched it, it swung back on its heavy hinges, and they found themselves in a little low room, with a vaulted ceiling, and one tiny grated window. Imbedded in the wall was a huge iron ring, and chained to it was a gaunt skeleton, that was stretched out at full length on the stone floor, and seemed to be trying to grasp with its long fleshless fingers an old-fashioned trencher and ewer, that were placed just out of its reach. The jug had evidently been once filled with water, as it was covered inside with green mould. There was nothing on the trencher but a pile of dust. Virginia knelt down beside the skeleton, and, folding her little hands together, began to pray silently, while the rest of the party looked on in wonder at the terrible tragedy whose secret was now disclosed to them.

"Hello!" suddenly exclaimed one of the twins, who had been looking out of the window to try and discover in what wing of the house the room was situated. "Hello! The old withered almond tree has blossomed. I can see the flowers quite plainly in the moonlight."

"God has forgiven him," said Virginia, gravely, as she rose to her feet, and a beautiful light seemed to illumine her face.

"What an angel you are!" cried the young Duke, and he put his arm round her neck, and kissed her.

VII

Four days after these curious incidents, a funeral started from Canterville Chase at about eleven o'clock at night. The hearse was drawn by eight black horses, each of which carried on its head a great tuft of nodding ostrich-plumes, and the leaden coffin was covered by a rich purple pall, on which was embroidered in gold the Canterville coat-of-arms. By the side of the hearse and the coaches walked the servants with lighted torches, and the whole procession was wonderfully impressive. Lord Canterville was the chief mourner, having come up specially from Wales to attend the funeral, and sat in the first carriage along with little Virginia. Then came the United States Minister and his wife, then Washington and the three boys, and in the last carriage was Mrs. Umney. It was generally felt that, as she had been frightened by the ghost for more than fifty years of her life, she had a right to see the last of him. A deep grave had been dug in the corner of the churchyard, just under the old yew tree, and the service was read in the most impressive manner by the Rev. Augustus Dampier. When the ceremony was over, the servants, according to an old custom observed in the Canterville family, extinguished their torches, and, as the coffin was being lowered into the grave, Virginia stepped forward, and laid on it a large cross made of white and pink almond-blossoms. As she did so, the moon came out from behind a cloud, and flooded with its silent silver the little churchyard, and from a distant copse a nightingale began to sing. She thought of the ghost's description of the Garden of Death, her eyes became dim with tears, and she hardly spoke a word during the drive home.

The next morning, before Lord Canterville went up to town, Mr. Otis had an interview with him on the subject of the jewels the ghost had given to Virginia. They were perfectly magnificent, especially a certain ruby necklace with old Venetian setting, which was really a superb specimen of sixteenth-century work, and their value was so great that Mr. Otis felt considerable scruples about allowing his daughter to accept them.

"My lord," he said, "I know that in this country mortmain is held to apply to trinkets as well as to land, and it is quite clear to me that these jewels are, or should be, heirlooms in your family. I must beg you, accordingly, to take them to London with you, and to regard them simply as a portion of your property which has been restored to you under certain strange conditions. As for my daughter, she is merely a child, and has as yet, I am glad to say, but little interest in such appurtenances of idle luxury. I am also informed by Mrs. Otis, who, I may say, is no mean authority upon Art,—having had the privilege of spending several winters in Boston when she was a girl,—that these gems are of great monetary worth, and if offered for sale would fetch a tall price. Under these circumstances, Lord Canterville, I feel sure that you will recognize how impossible it would be for me to allow them to remain in the possession of any member of my family; and, indeed, all such vain gauds and toys, however suitable or necessary to the dignity of the British aristocracy, would be completely out of place among those who have been brought up on the severe, and I believe immortal, principles of Republican simplicity. Perhaps I should mention that Virginia is very anxious that you should allow her to retain the box, as a memento of your unfortunate but misguided ancestor. As it is extremely old, and consequently a good deal out of repair, you may perhaps think fit to comply with her request. For my own part, I confess I am a good deal surprised to find a child of mine expressing sympathy with medievalism in any form, and can only account for it by the fact that Virginia was born in one of your London suburbs shortly after Mrs. Otis had returned from a trip to Athens."

Lord Canterville listened very gravely to the worthy

Minister's speech, pulling his grey moustache now and then to hide an involuntary smile, and when Mr. Otis had ended, he shook him cordially by the hand, and said: "My dear sir, your charming little daughter rendered my unlucky ancestor, Sir Simon, a very important service, and I and my family are much indebted to her for her marvellous courage and pluck. The jewels are clearly hers, and, egad, I believe that if I were heartless enough to take them from her, the wicked old fellow would be out of his grave in a fortnight, leading me the devil of a life. As for their being heirlooms, nothing is an heirloom that is not so mentioned in a will or legal document, and the existence of these jewels has been quite unknown. I assure you I have no more claim on them than your butler, and when Miss Virginia grows up, I dare say she will be pleased to have pretty things to wear. Besides, you forget, Mr. Otis, that you took the furniture and the ghost at a valuation, and anything that belonged to the ghost passed at once into your possession, as, whatever activity Sir Simon may have shown in the corridor at night, in point of law he was really dead, and you acquired his property by purchase."

Mr. Otis was a good deal distressed at Lord Canterville's refusal, and begged him to reconsider his decision, but the good-natured peer was quite firm, and finally induced the Minister to allow his daughter to retain the present the ghost had given her, and when, in the spring of 1890, the young Duchess of Cheshire was presented at the Queen's first drawing room on the occasion of her marriage, her jewels were the universal theme of admiration. For Virginia received the coronet, which is the reward of all good little American girls, and was married to her boy-lover as soon as he came of age. They were both so charming, and they loved each other so much, that everyone was delighted at the match, except the old Marchioness of Dumbleton, who had tried to catch the Duke for one of her seven unmarried daughters, and had given no less than three expensive dinner parties for that purpose, and, strange to say, Mr. Otis himself. Mr. Otis was extremely fond of the young Duke personally, but, theoretically, he objected to titles, and, to use his own words, "was not without apprehension lest, amid the enervating influences of a pleasure-loving aristocracy, the true principles of Republican simplicity should be forgotten." His objections, however, were completely overruled, and I believe that when he walked up the aisle of St. George's, Hanover Square, with his daughter leaning on his arm, there was not a prouder man in the whole length and breadth of England.

The Duke and Duchess, after the honeymoon was over, went down to Canterville Chase, and on the day after their arrival they walked over in the afternoon to the lonely churchyard by the pine woods. There had been a great deal of difficulty at first about the inscription on Sir Simon's tombstone, but finally it had been decided to engrave on it simply the initials of the old gentleman's name, and the verse from the library window. The Duchess had brought with her some lovely roses, which she strewed upon the grave, and after they had stood by it for some time they strolled into the ruined chancel of the old abbey. There the Duchess sat down on a fallen pillar, while her husband lay at her feet smoking a cigarette and looking up at her beautiful eyes. Suddenly he threw his cigarette away, took hold of her hand, and said to her, "Virginia, a wife should have no secrets from her husband."

"Dear Cecil! I have no secrets from you."

"Yes, you have," he answered, smiling, "you have never told me what happened to you when you were locked up with the ghost."

"I have never told anyone, Cecil," said Virginia, gravely.

"I know that, but you might tell me."

"Please don't ask me, Cecil, I cannot tell you. Poor Sir Simon! I owe him a great deal. Yes, don't laugh, Cecil, I really do. He made me see what Life is, and what Death signifies, and why Love is stronger than both."

The Duke rose and kissed his wife lovingly.

"You can have your secret as long as I have your heart," he murmured.

"You have always had that, Cecil."

"And you will tell our children some day, won't you?"

Virginia blushed.